Maura's Angel

Maura's Angel

LYNNE REID BANKS

AN AVON CAMELOT BOOK

AVON BOOKS, INC.
1350 Avenue of the Americas
New York, New York 10019

Copyright © 1984 by Lynne Reid Banks
Published by arrangement with the author
Library of Congress Catalog Card Number: 97-50350
ISBN: 0-380-79514-0
www.avonbooks.com

First Avon Camelot Printing: April 1999
First Avon Camelot Hardcover Printing: May 1998

CAMELOT TRADEMARK REG. U.S. PAT. OFF. AND IN OTHER COUNTRIES, MARCA REGISTRADA, HECHO EN U.S.A.

Printed in the U.S.A.

OPM 10 9 8 7 6 5 4 3 2 1

For Mary, Susan, Rich,
Linda, Dwain, and John M.

Maura's Angel

One

THE REASON MAURA fell asleep during school assembly that Thursday morning was because she was honestly tired. And small wonder—she'd been up half the night with her baby brother Darren.

Her mother had said *she* couldn't anymore, she just wasn't able. And Maura, looking at her poor, thin, tired face, saw it was true. So she told her ma to go back to bed. She picked Darren up, and walked him, and gave him his bottle of sweet tea, but still he didn't go to sleep for hours.

And she'd had to get up early in the morning to get six-year-old Foley, whose real name was Paul, ready for school and take him (it was only around the corner), and then dress her sister Colleen.

Colleen was nineteen, but she couldn't dress herself properly, or do anything else properly, even talk. Maura had got her nicely sat up to table and given her her porridge (heated up from yesterday), and taken her ma a cup of tea in bed, hoping she'd wake up and come down and help. She didn't. She was out like a light. Luckily, the baby was sleeping off his late night, too. When he woke up and started howling, Ma would have to stir herself.

Just as Maura was dashing out the door to catch the bus to school, she heard Colleen's tin dish clatter to the floor . . . She paused, and then, guiltily, ran on, pretending she hadn't heard. It was pointless to feel annoyed with Colleen. She couldn't help it. But Maura couldn't help some things either, such as thinking it was a pity to have wasted the last of the porridge on Colleen only to have her knock it all over the floor. But she felt guilty just the same. She should have stopped to wipe it up! Ma would be in no mood . . .

As she hurried along the short, narrow street where she lived, with its front doors and front windows opening straight on to the pavement, Maura glanced, as she always did, at the words written up on the walls. Most of them had been there for so long that it was surprising she still noticed them, but they held a strange sort of magic for her. She'd got into the habit of reading them every morning, and had a fear (she knew it was silly) that if she missed one day, something bad would happen.

Parts of Belfast, Maura's city, were scrawled all over. Even the mailboxes weren't red anymore, but black and white with paint-writing. It was as if the people who lived here in Northern Ireland were trying to make their feelings known to the world in the only way they felt able to—very angry feelings.

Of course there was plenty of ordinary, pointless sort of wall-writing, names and so on; but Maura never bothered looking at those. The words that she superstitiously read every time she passed were things like: IT'S NOT YOUR SON BUT WHAT IF IT WAS? and, GIVE THEM THEIR RIGHTS NOT THEIR LAST RITES. These referred to men in prison on hunger-strike.

Still another she always read was SOLDIER GO HOME. She saw that everywhere, not just in her street. Another said, DON'T THINK THE TOUTS WILL STOP US.

This one gave Maura a little shiver—touts were informers, and Maura had good reason to hate them: due to one tout, her big brother had been shut away for ten years.

Where her little street turned into the main road, there was something special. The whole end-wall of the last house was one big painting.

Maura had seen it so often it was imprinted on her mind. It showed a young man lying in a prison bed, his rosary in his limp hand; the Virgin Mary stood above him with pools of yellow light falling over him from her halo.

The man's face was spoiled. Someone had come along one night and thrown a whole tin of black paint at it. But Maura remembered it from before. She knew the picture had to do with men going on hunger-strike in the Maze Prison, outside the city.

Kieran, Maura's twenty-one-year-old brother, was a prisoner there, though he had not been part of the hunger-strike (it had happened just before he was taken).

Sometimes she dreamed of Kieran with a black face, like the wall-painting, but more like a photo she'd seen once of a tout who'd been covered with tar for a punishment. She had no pact with herself to look at the picture, and, as it upset her, she didn't. But she always glanced above it to read the words, carefully painted with a brush, not sprayed or scrawled: BLESSED ARE THEY THAT HUNGER FOR JUSTICE.

Maura had lived the whole of her eleven years in a city at war—at war with itself. It showed. It showed in the stories in the papers and on TV, in the soldiers with their camouflage uniforms and guns patrolling the streets, in the things that Maura actually saw and heard sometimes—furious, ugly things. Most of all, perhaps, it showed in the wall-writing and painting.

But Maura wasn't afraid of the signs of violence and anger all around her. She should have been, perhaps, but she wasn't. She was too used to it. She took it for granted, except when something exceptional happened, as it was going to that very day, if Maura had only known it.

She had to go to school on a bus. She often wished she could go to a school closer to home, like Foley, but her mother had been to St. Vincent's and wanted Maura to go there too. So every morning she waited at the bus-stop. Sometimes if the bus was late, she took one of the old black taxis instead—not a private taxi, a shared one which cost the same or less than a bus, though her mother didn't like her taking a taxi. The seat-coverings were old and often split and Ma had an idea she might "pick up" some bug from them. Needless to say, Maura loved the taxis, partly because they were sort of forbidden; but this morning she had no excuse to take one. The bus came within a few minutes.

The farther it carried her from home, the more her home-problems faded and the more she thought forward to school. Maura liked school. Sister Josephine, the principal, was very old, very strict, and often short-tempered, but most of the teachers were young and nice. The other children were all right too (on the whole—there were exceptions, such as Eileen O'Malley). Although Maura found the lessons hard enough to make her very anxious about moving next year to secondary school, thinking about them gave her a rest from thinking about all her worries at home.

In the cloakroom she hung up her raincoat over the top of her two bags, one for books and one for sports things. They weren't allowed to take anything into assembly; the "hall" wasn't big enough for anything but the two hundred girls. They went to their classrooms for registration, and then they all filed into the "hall," actually a double classroom which was also the gym. There were no posters or pictures hung on the walls because of all the apparatus, just the big crucifix between the main windows at the far end, where Sister Josephine was waiting. Because it was the saint's day of their school, Father Brady had come specially to talk to them.

Maura sat down with all the others on her own little carpet-mat on the polished floor. Luckily she was sitting beside fat Patty, who was like a lovely, padded backrest. Maura edged her mat along the hard floor until she could lean against Patty, and almost as soon as Sister Josephine started talking, she nodded off.

She woke up for the hymn, though. Patty chose it because it was her birthday as well as Saint Vincent's, and it was "All Things Bright and Beautiful." Maura sang louder than anyone—she loved to sing, and she couldn't very well at home, because Colleen was apt to join in any kind of music, which was enough to put anyone off. Maura sang all the verses at the top of her voice and then fell asleep again.

She only woke up this time when Patty nudged her.

"Father Brady's got his beady eye on you," she whispered.

Maura sat up straight and tried to look devout and attentive.

"So keep it in mind," the father was saying. "You're never alone as long as they are with you, and, as they're always with you, sure you're never alone." He beamed around the hall at all of them.

"Who are?" Maura whispered to Patty.

"Shhhh!"

"It's their job, you see," Father Brady was saying.

"Their God-given assignment. They've nothing else in the world or the heavens to trouble themselves about, except one or the other of you. To listen til' your prayers, to guide you in the ways you should go, to carry your messages til' Our Lady, and in general, to look after you. So you see," he wound up, his hands comfortably resting on his big tummy, "even in these troubled times, there's nothing to fear. Even if the good Lord might be a bit too busy to be keeping His Holy Eye on you every minute of the day, you can rest assured: *there's always your guardian angel.*"

Maura could not help giving a little sniff. Was that so? And where was her guardian angel when the going got rough? Where was he when the soldiers had come for Kieran? Maura had prayed as hard as ever she could that they'd let him off and not put him in the Maze, but they had. What was her guardian angel doing about her prayers, every single night—on the cold floor, mind you, not in bed—that her da, who'd gone off with the Provos, would come home so her ma wouldn't be so lonely? Come to that, what about the time her other brother, Patrick, had had the meningitis and screamed and screamed?

All right, she thought, maybe an angel couldn't do everything. But she'd sent up a prayer or two last night that Darren would just stop his yelling and let her get some sleep. That wasn't asking much, surely. Where was her guardian angel *then?* Asleep himself, maybe, if angels did sleep. Anyway, not on the job so's you'd notice it, that was for certain.

*   *   *

She dozed through the rest of the day, only waking up for games and geography. You couldn't sleep through games, and in geography they were drawing maps, which she liked, especially coloring them. She put a thick blue scribbly border with her crayon round the coasts and then borrowed Kathleen's black felt-tip to outline the countries. This made them all stand out beautifully, and she got a merit mark for it, the first for two weeks. Then she was given a detention for putting her head down on her desk in math, but the teacher took it off again when she explained about her baby brother.

So that was a fairly average day, up until school ended and she was walking along the side-street to the bus-stop on her own. Then it happened. The start of it all. A really shattering great bang from the main street just around the corner, the loudest noise Maura had ever heard in her life.

She found herself flat on her face on the pavement. Whether she threw herself down or whether the blast knocked her over, she didn't know; she was just there. For some moments there was nothing, just blackness and a breathless silence, and the hard stone beneath her stomach and bruises on her knees.

This was not the first time, so she knew what it was—it was a bomb. Last time it had not gone off so near her, though. She hadn't been so frightened that time, not when it happened. Later, when she got home, she was sick. That was after the soldier had picked her up.

Would a soldier try to pick her up this time? It was the only time she had ever let one near her. Kieran, before they put him in prison, had told her, and so had her da, "Never go near the Brits and never let them near you." Maybe that was what had made her throw up, remembering his clumsy hands lifting her by the arms and dusting her down and his English voice saying, "Go 'ome, girlie. No—not that way, it's nasty. Go round the back alley."

She felt a little movement at her side. Was it a soldier? She lifted her head above her arm and peeped.

Then she jerked her head up higher and goggled.

It wasn't a soldier. It was a girl, lying right beside her, on her stomach like Maura and with her face buried in her arms. And she was bare.

Totally, absolutely bare. She hadn't a stitch on her. The only way Maura knew she was a girl and not a boy was because of her hair, which was long and shiny and in curls. It was just the same color as Maura's own, but much prettier. (And much cleaner.)

Maura was so shocked at the bareness that she forgot to be surprised or to wonder where the girl had come from.

"Why aren't you dressed?" she asked in a scandalized tone.

The other girl moved her head sharply and looked up at her. Then Maura got the strangest feeling. It was like looking in a mirror. No. Not quite. This girl was like her, but not exactly. Staring and staring, fascinated, Maura saw several differences, apart from the hair.

The other girl's mouth was hanging open a bit and Maura could see that her teeth were perfectly straight, unlike her own, which were crooked. Her eyes—the other girl's—were wide open and clear, clear blue, not red-rimmed and bunged-up with sleepiness like Maura's. And she didn't have Maura's little scar on her cheek from where she'd fallen downstairs when she was three.

And her skin was different. It was so pale and clean it was almost white. The girl was . . . well, beautiful. She was like a perfectly beautiful Maura.

"You're undressed," Maura said again, reproachfully. Somehow this was still the most important thing. She'd had it well drilled into her that nakedness was sinful. None of them at home would ever be more than half-undressed before any of the others after they were about two years old.

The other girl didn't say anything. She looked dazed. Maura wondered fleetingly whether the blast from the bomb had blown her clothes clean off her, and looked down anxiously at herself. But no. All her own clothes were still decently in place.

She scrambled to her feet, looking around. There were noises now, shouting and sirens, and that funny smoky smell, creeping around the corner from where the bomb had gone off. It must have been somewhere near the bus-stop! She longed to go and look. But the other girl was still lying there. She couldn't just leave her.

"Come on, get up! I'll lend you my coat."

She peeled it off, just as an ambulance screamed

around another corner and raced past. Instinctively Maura threw her coat over the other girl so the driver wouldn't see.

"Why aren't you dressed?" she asked again.

The girl was climbing to her feet. She didn't move beautifully. She moved as if she didn't know how to make her body do what she wanted it to.

She stood for a moment, opening and closing her mouth. The coat hung off one shoulder, all lopsided, and she didn't even move her hands to wrap it around her.

"I—don't—know," she said in a strange voice with a sort of tinkle in it, like a wee silver bell.

Maura gazed at her for a moment longer. Well, she thought, at least she hasn't got my *voice*. Then, impatiently, as she might have done with Foley, she pulled the coat straight and did some buttons up. But although she was now covered, the girl's arms were not in the sleeves. She was like a raincoat-parcel. Maura pulled it off again and, glancing around nervously, pushed the limp arms into the sleeves and buttoned it up again. Two snowy-white legs and little delicate feet stuck out at the bottom.

Maura looked at those feet. She often went barefoot herself at home in the summer, and her own feet were rather calloused and often grubby. These feet . . . well, they shouldn't be touching a dirty, hard pavement, that was all Maura knew! They looked as if they'd never, ever touched anything dirty or hard.

Maura had a sudden idea. She looked around. Yes, there was her bag of books, and there her sports bag, lying where they had fallen. She grabbed the sports bag and, prising it open with her fingers without bothering to undo the tape, fished out first one gymshoe and then the other.

"You'd better be puttin' these on."

The girl looked at them, then back at Maura again. She didn't seem to know what she meant.

Suddenly, Maura thought she understood. Of course! This girl was not bright. Like her big sister Colleen.

Maura knew all about not-bright people—how could she not, with Colleen in the house? She'd been doing things for Colleen ever since she herself could toddle. And she knew other not-bright people, too, from the center where Colleen sometimes spent a day to give their mother a break from looking after her.

This girl certainly looked nothing like Colleen. She didn't *look* not-bright—she just didn't have the look. The opposite, in fact. She actually looked more than bright, she seemed to shine . . . But she must be wrong in her head or she wouldn't just stand there with all that racket going on just around the corner. People were now beginning to come out of their houses and rush past them (thank the Lord Maura'd managed to get the coat around the girl, anyhow!). But she was not taking a bit of notice of the row, just staring and staring at Maura.

"Come here wit' you. Sit down on this step."

Maura thought it best to treat her as she treated Colleen. She manhandled her firmly to the step and pressed on her shoulders. The girl sank down, still gazing up at her helplessly. Maura capably slipped first one gymshoe and then the other onto those little soft white feet. The girl's face looked puzzled as she glanced down. Then, seeing the old plimsolls at the ends of her legs, she stuck her legs straight out, and suddenly laughed.

Then she clapped her hands over her mouth and looked at Maura in a scared way.

"It's okay now," said Maura reassuringly. "You're decent. And I must catch my bus. That's if there's a bus-stop left to catch it at!" She listened for a minute to the growing roar from the bomb-site. "Do you have to be home?" she asked. The girl slowly shook her head. On an irresistible impulse, Maura caught the other girl's hand and pulled her up. "Come on! Let's go see the bomb!" she cried, and the next minute they were both running.

Two

RUNNING WITH THIS other girl was strange, somehow. She kept stumbling. Once she almost fell; Maura had to stop, turn and grab her. Her face was now not just beautifully pale but deathly white, her eyes were popping and she was gasping for breath like fat Patty, who had asthma.

"Are you all right?"

The girl nodded, but she didn't look all right. Maura decided to slow down, but it was frustrating. The street was full of people, all running in one direction, and Maura longed to run, too. But she was held back by the girl, who now walked along slowly and carefully, watching her feet in their black canvas gymshoes as if marveling at how they moved.

She *must* be not-bright, Maura thought, trying to be patient.

They rounded the corner. A chaotic scene met their

eyes. A big crowd of people, all with their backs to them; a jam of police cars, ambulances and a fire-engine; lots of noise and confusion, and the smoke. Maura looked for the bus-stop sticking out of the crowd, but couldn't see it.

"Come on, let's get closer!"

She pulled the girl into the back of the crowd, squirming and wriggling to get through, but the girl again delayed her. It was like dragging a dead weight—no squirming and wriggling for her, she just stayed upright and let Maura lug her along like a sack of coal on legs.

Maura's head popped out between two people in the front of the crowd and she found herself practically in the arms of a policeman.

"Oh no you don't! The two of yez get out of here, and quick about it, this is no place for wee girls!"

He tried to turn her back into the crowd, but the narrow gap she had forced for herself had closed up. The people were like a solid mass. The other girl stood there in front of a man in a dark raincoat. Against this, her face looked unnaturally pale, like an old painting of the Madonna that Maura had seen in a book. Skin, she had thought scornfully at the time, simply wasn't that color.

The policeman, too, was staring at the girl.

"You'd best be getting *her* home, and yourself with her. Come on, I'll clear you a path through them'ns."

But Maura wasn't listening. She had caught a glimpse, beyond him, of what he was trying to stop her seeing.

The front of the café opposite her bus-stop, into which she had often peeped at the wee tables under their red cloths, and the nice things to eat, was no more. The crackly bits of glass under her feet were all that was left of the big window. The tables and chairs had been flung everywhere. All their neat, checkered tablecloths, and cups and plates and knives and forks and salts-and-peppers were gone. There was nothing but a great black hole with flames around its edges. There were policemen trying to push the crowd back, and firemen trying to force their way through with a hose.

And there were other things. Terrible things.

Maura glimpsed all this in the few seconds she was allowed to look at it. Then she heard a sound from behind her. It was the same sort of noise Patrick had made when he was in pain from the meningitis and it got too bad even to let him yell. A kind of whimpering moan.

She turned. The girl who looked like her was bent double, her arms over her head.

"Sure, I knew it, she's not well," said the constable. "And who can wonder! Come on now, move away wit' yez, let the services through." He began to shout. "Let the wee girls out! Move, move, or I'll call the sergeant—"

Parting the crowd with great heaves of his shoulder, he forced his way through like a crab, dragging the girls along, holding their two hands in one of his. The crowd reluctantly parted to let them through, but closed again behind them. Maura thought, This time I'm not going to get home before I throw up. I'm going to throw up here and now.

And she did, just as soon as she got in sight of the gutter.

Feeling better, she stood upright and looked around. The policeman had gone off somewhere. The street was getting more crowded, noisy and confused every moment. The girl stood by her, hugging her head. Not looking at anything. Colleen hadn't acted like this when they saw that dead soldier when they were coming home from the center. She just pointed at him and laughed.

"Hey," Maura said, not as gently as she'd meant to, "come on." She pulled an arm down, and tried to peer into her face. The girl turned it away. It was all twisted and screwed up. She was trembling all over like a wet dog.

"Where d'you live?"

No answer.

"I'll take you to your home and you can give me back my coat and gymshoes. I'll catch a hit from my ma if I come home without them."

The girl moved then. She tried to take the coat off there and then.

"Will you stop that?" cried Maura, shocked. "Before all these people! Don't you know where you live?" She gave the frail-feeling arm a bit of a shake.

The girl looked at her and opened and shut her mouth, like a fish.

"I live—" she began in that tinkling voice, only it was all shaky now, "I live with you," she said.

"With *me?* What d'you mean by that?"

"I live with you."

"The devil you do!" said Maura, talking like Kieran used to. She gazed at her companion. "What's your name?"

"I don't—"

"Don't tell me you don't know that! Even Colleen knows her own name!"

"Colleen?"

"My big sister that's simple in the head. She's not-bright, like you."

"Not-bright?" Suddenly the twisted-up face cleared and the girl opened her mouth, and right there in the street among all the smoke and racket she began to sing a hymn! The same one as in assembly that morning.

"All things bright and beautiful, all creatures great and small—All things wise and—"

Maura shook her arm again and pushed her into a rapid walk. "Will you shut up? You'll make people think you're loony!"

The girl walked along docilely beside her. She walked more smoothly now and after a bit she stopped watching her feet all the time, and glanced ahead. Her red lips moved. Maura put her head closer. She was mouthing the words of the hymn silently to herself.

Yes. This was like Colleen. Colleen loved to sing and she didn't care where she was or who heard her. That was why they couldn't take her to Mass. She'd be likely to start singing a pop song right in the middle of the service. She hadn't a singing voice like this one, though. It all came out muddly with Colleen.

"Is my name Maura?"

Maura stopped dead. A shiver of fear went up her back.

"How'd you know I'm called Maura?" she asked fiercely.

The girl looked at her with her deep blue eyes, so like Maura's own, and yet, not like. These were more like Darren's eyes. A baby's eyes which have never seen anything but loving faces. But there was already a little shadow in them which hadn't been there at first.

"Are we both called Maura?" She gave a sudden, sweet smile which melted Maura's fears and her anger, but not her puzzlement.

"Are you playing games with me? Who are you, anyhow?"

"Don't *you* know me?" asked the girl.

Maura shook her head. They were standing in another street now, one that was nearly empty. An army lorry full of Brits roared by in the direction of the bomb. Maura and the girl watched it go.

"Brits go home," muttered Maura automatically. Then she heaved a deep sigh and her face broke into its normal expression—a cheerful grin. "And *Maura* go home. Come on, what are we standing here for? My ma will have my guts for garters!"

She turned and began to run. She half hoped the other girl would not follow, but she did. She ran badly, but she ran, and even though Maura could easily have left her far behind, "lost" her in fact, she somehow couldn't. As she drew ahead, it was as if something pulled her back. She stopped, sighed in exasperation, and stood and waited.

The girl reached her, and drooped, panting, before her.

"You're not much of a runner, are you," said Maura.

"I'm not used to using them."

"What?"

"Those," she pointed downwards. "My—" She paused for a moment as if to remember. "My feet." She gave that breathy little laugh again. "They look so funny in those black things."

"How do you usually walk about then?" asked Maura sarcastically.

"I don't usually—walk about," said the girl.

There was a silence. She was crazy for sure, this one.

"Well," said Maura finally, "I've to go home straight. I suppose I'll have to take you with me. Then we can find out who you belong to."

They waited at another bus-stop for a while but then Maura decided that there probably were no buses because of the bomb. Instead Maura hailed a black taxi. There were four people in it already but they squeezed in on one back-to-front seat. As they went along, Maura tried various names on her companion.

"Would you fancy being a Mary?" she whispered, so their fellow-passengers wouldn't hear.

"Oh, no!"

"Why 'Oh no!'? There's loads of Marys."

"Only one," said the girl strangely.

"Well, then. What about—Cathleen? That's my ma's name."

The girl shook her head.

"Maureen? That's like mine."

"No."

"Well, what then? You say."

"I don't know about names." After a long silence, she suddenly said, "Michael."

Maura smothered a giggle. "Silly! That's a boy's name."

"Are they different?"

Maura blushed. "Sure they're very different. Don't you know anything?"

"I know there are—males and females. But I don't—know how they're different. Their souls are the same."

The girl didn't seem to know about whispering. The other people in the taxi exchanged embarrassed glances. Maura blushed and turned her head away. To hear a girl of her own age talking like a nun or a priest made her feel all queer again.

And she was getting very worried about what her mother would say when she got home. It would be almost too late to get to the shops, normally her first job after school. And if Colleen had been acting up, or Darren, or if Foley came home dirty from school, their mother would be in a mood.

Three

SHE WAS IN a mood, but not in the way Maura had expected.

As the girls reached the front door of the little row house in the narrow street, it flew open and a red, shiny arm shot out, grabbed Maura and pulled her across the threshold. She cringed, expecting a cuff on the head—not a very hard one. Her mother had neither the strength nor the wish to hurt her seriously. But this time there was no cuffing. Instead she found herself clutched tightly against her mother's apron-bib, listening to the wobbly beating of her heart.

"Oh, praise be to God you're all right! Oh, Jesus, Mary and Joseph, I've been almost out of my wits!"

Maura submitted to her hug out of surprise, because it was rather a rare experience since her da disappeared. Her da used to hug and kiss all of them, all the time—even Colleen. Big overgrown poor thing

that she was, he used to take her on his knee . . .
But he loved Maura best and there were lots of cuddles and love from him. Her mother was different.

"What's wrong, Ma?"

"What's wrong? *What's wrong?* With bombs going off to left and right, just near the school, what would you think might be wrong?" Her mother had been crying, Maura could see. "Mrs. Dooley came in with the news—it nearly finished me off, so it did." Her voice took on a wailing note which Maura knew all too well. "Oh, will it never stop? Will it never end? Are we never to know any peace and an end to misery and worry?"

With one arm still tightly wrapped around Maura's shoulders, she shut the front door behind them without even noticing the other girl on the doorstep.

"Ma—there's—"

Her mother abruptly left off wailing and got back to normal.

"Well, since you're all right, you can just lend a hand now. You've no need to shop; I sent Foley after the bread and tea and we can manage for the rest till tomorrow. Get on upstairs now and change the baby if he's awake, and see if you can't straighten the bedrooms a bit. Here, take the sweeper with you. Oh," she added as Maura began climbing the stairs, clutching the heavy carpet-sweeper, "the washing-machine's on the bum again. Put the washing in the bath and give it a good swish around with the bath-brush. Lots of Daz, mind, and hot water. No, wait!" Maura, suppressing a sigh, stopped. "Run the bath full and before you put in the clothes, see if you can't get Colleen in, she hasn't had a proper wash for a week. . . . Then do the wash in the same water. I'll call you when dinner's ready."

Maura toiled out of sight around the stair-bend.

"Maura . . . !" Her mother's voice sounded different, gentler. Maura poked her head around the post.

"What, Ma?"

Her mother was looking up at her with anxious, weary eyes.

"Nothin' at all . . . It's just . . . I was afraid for you. Sure, I don't know what I'd have done if you'd come to any harm."

Da would have said, "I love you, Maurabelle."

Upstairs on the dark, cluttered landing, Maura thought, If I don't do anything about that wee girl, p'raps she'll go away. She didn't know if she wanted her to go or stay, but the thought of her staying was too difficult. Her mother (as she often said) had enough on her plate, and wouldn't welcome strangers, especially one with nothing on under her—or rather, Maura's—raincoat. On the other hand, if she went off, taking the coat with her, what would Ma have to say about *that*?

Oh, well—out of sight, out of mind. Maura got on with her chores. She ran the bath first (Darren was still asleep) and then led Colleen in from their small shared bedroom where, as usual, she had been sitting half-asleep beside the window. Colleen was glad to see her and made her welcoming faces and noises, but she wasn't glad to see the bath, full of hot, steamy water.

"Na—naaaa—Collnaaaaa . . ." she whined.

"Maura's got a sweetie," Maura chipped in quickly.

"Sweecoll?" Colleen asked, full of hope.

"Bathies first," said Maura firmly, and began to take Colleen's clothes off.

This was no easy task. Colleen was very fat and she hated to be uncovered. Body-warmth was important to her. This meant that the bath itself would be a pleasure, once she got into it. The trouble was, she never remembered that, she just felt the cold air on her skin, and she resisted and moaned and even tried to flee as the layers of clothes came off.

But Maura didn't give up and she was at last rewarded by a long, happy sigh of "Aaaaaaah!" as she eased her sister into the warm water.

After that it was plain sailing. Maura gave Colleen her bath-toys and her sweet and even let her have one of her own precious Christmas bath-pearls, a red one (Colleen loved red and she loved nice smells) to squidge and melt in the water and watch the oil squirt out. Then Maura was free to go off and tend to Darren, who by this time had woken up and was yelling his head off.

Darren was gorgeous. Even red in the face and sopping wet, he was the loveliest baby in the world. Maura soon stopped the yelling with a cuddle, stuck a dummy in his mouth, changed him expertly into a nice dry nappy and some clean pants, and carried him into the room she shared with Colleen.

It was in the front of the house and, carrying him

to the window so he could look at the big world of the street outside, she suddenly noticed a forlorn little figure on the pavement below, staring up at her.

Oh Lord!

Maura opened the window and leaned out, holding Darren tight.

"Knock on the door and tell my ma you're a friend come to play!" she whispered down as loudly as she dared.

"Knock?" came the silvery voice.

"Yes, silly—knock!" And Maura demonstrated in the air. The girl looked down at her own hand, then rolled her fingers up carefully into a fist. It wasn't a very tight fist and made hardly any noise on the wood.

"Use the knocker!" hissed Maura.

The girl seemed to get the idea and lifted the knocker, letting it fall back with a bang. Maura, with a strange sense of foreboding, heard her mother go to the door, and saw it open.

"And what can I do for—" her mother's sharpest voice began.

Then she stopped.

"Holy Mother of God!" Maura heard her exclaim softly.

There was a silence. Then the girl, after glancing upward, said, "I'm-a-friend-and-I've-come-to-play," all in one breath.

Maura expected her mother to say, "She's too busy," or "Come back later," as she often did when friends came during what her da had called "business hours"—the times when she was helping at home. But this time was different. Her mother backed out of the doorway and Maura saw the girl walking in through it.

She rushed back to Ma's and Darren's room, dumped Darren, who was outraged, into his cot, and ran downstairs.

Her mother was in a state! She was standing in the narrow hallway with the door still wide open, staring at the strange girl as if she were seeing ghosts.

"Ma, this is my friend," said Maura quickly. "I— I met her near school. She—I think she got a bit of a fright when the bomb went off, but she'll be fine if we can just help her a wee bit."

She expected her mother to wake up at that and take some action, even if it was only to say it was nothing to do with them and she'd be thankful if Maura wouldn't put any more on her plate. But all her mother did was look, first at the girl, and then at Maura, and then back again at the girl. Her face was strained and white and her mouth was hanging open. And all of a sudden, she burst into tears.

"Ma! What's wrong? She's only a poor wee girl. Sure it's nothing to cry for!" Maura said, rushing to embrace her mother. She was frightened. The last time Ma had cried aloud like that had been when those men came and persuaded Da to go away with them, and the time before that had been at Patrick's funeral. (She hadn't cried for Kieran going to the Maze. She had been too angry.)

"It's my baby! It's my baby!" her mother kept saying. "Oh, it can't be—what am I sayin'—it can't be—she's dead and gone, poor wee soul—but oh my God, how like you she is! How could anything be so like?"

Maura couldn't calm her. After a few minutes of trying, she left her and ran into the kitchen. In the cupboard beneath the sink there was hidden a bottle half-full of whisky. It had been Da's secret supply, not touched since he'd gone. Maura poured some into a mug and took it to her mother.

But in those few seconds, something had happened. Her mother had not only stopped crying (except for that hiccupping you always get afterwards) but was actually smiling. The color had come back to her thin cheeks, so much, in fact, that it looked like rouge. The girl was standing close to her and had one of her thin, white hands on her arm.

Maura stopped in the kitchen doorway, looking at them. She felt something small and sharp stabbing at her heart. *She* hadn't been able to quieten her mother. This stranger had done it with one touch! Never mind, though. Ma looked better, that was the main thing.

"D'you want a drop of the drink, Ma?"

Her mother turned. She had a funny, blank look for a moment.

"What, Maura?—Oh! Heavens above, no, take the filthy stuff out of my sight and throw it down the sink! No, wait. Get the funnel and pour it back in the bottle. You never know when your da will come home and be askin' for it."

She was her ordinary self again, leading the strange girl briskly into the kitchen.

"You look as if you could do with some tea," she was saying. "Sit down now and I'll get you something. Maura! Don't just stand there. Go out the back and call Foley. He'll be playin' in the alley."

"Couldn't you, Ma? He won't come in for me."

"Oh, all right then. You make this one a fry and a strong cup of tea. Put some color in her cheeks . . ." She paused, and, as if she couldn't help it, drew one rough red finger down the girl's cheek. "Will you only look at that skin, it's like a camellia's petals . . ." Tears threatened her eyes again, but she turned quickly and went out the back door, calling in her normal, sharp-edged voice.

"Paul! Will you come in straight for your tea!" None of them ever called Foley "Paul" unless they were cross with him.

Four

MAURA PUT THE kettle on, laid some bacon in the frying-pan, and while it was cooking spread margarine on some bread and put it in front of the girl. She looked down at it, but made no move to touch it.

"Aren't you hungry?"

"I don't know."

"Well, I am!" said Maura, taking a monstrous bite out of her piece. The girl watched, fascinated, and, it seemed, almost shocked. Maura paused—maybe it *was* too big a bite. But still the girl stared.

"What's up wit' you? Never seen a person eat bread before?"

"No."

"Well, eat some yourself instead of gaping at me!"

The girl gingerly picked up her bread by one corner. The slice lolled from her finger and thumb, like a white tongue. Bending her head, the girl tried clumsily to get her mouth around it.

Maura tut-tutted like her mother.

"Just look at how you're managing! Even Colleen—OH!" She jumped up, hand to mouth. She'd forgotten all about Coll! "I must get her out of the bath and put the clothes in!"

But half-way to the door, she stopped and came back. "Here, I'll cut yours up for you," she said kindly. Swiftly she cut the soda-bread into squares as if for Darren, and even scraped some marmalade on to one. She turned down the gas under the bacon, which was already putting out lovely smells.

The girl sniffed the air. "I feel strange," she announced.

"How? Have you a pain?"

"Here," said the girl, laying a hand on the coat where it covered her stomach.

"Like a big hole?" The girl nodded solemnly. "Well, that's hunger. It wants you to fill it up. Here!" She pushed a little square of bread into the girl's mouth. "Now, chew! Like this," and she champed her jaws to show her.

A look of puzzlement and then of delight came over the pale face as she worked her jaws.

"You'll get used til' it," said Maura with a nod of satisfaction. "I'm gone upstairs. Will you call me if the bacon starts burning? I'll be back soon."

She didn't expect to be. Usually it took as long to get Colleen out of the bath as it had to get her into it. But this time the water was getting cold; Colleen was fretful and impatient for the rub with the warm towel in front of the little electric heater, her brushed-nylon nightie and dressing-gown, and the "swee" (her word for any kind of food) which always came next. She was cooperative, even putting her arms up nicely for her sleeves. She opened her mouth wide several times to show Maura that the first sweet was all gone, no doubt hoping for another, but Maura was firm.

"Dinner," she said, pointing Coll at the stairs.

Colleen obediently started down, holding the rail with both hands. She was not very happy about stairs; only the smell of bacon from below persuaded her to tackle them. Maura topped up the bath, added more Daz (she'd put in some to wash Coll) and collected all the dirty clothes from baskets and floors in the three little bedrooms.

In Foley's she glanced, as always, at Kieran's tidy, unused bed. It was always kept made up, and all his thing were on the shelves—his picture of Fidel Castro and Yasir Arafat kept nice for him. *What for?* a secret voice in Maura's head asked. Ten years they'd given Kieran, and only two of them past . . . He'd get some remission as a model prisoner, but not much . . . All his revolutionary heroes would probably be dead long before he was let out.

Darren started bawling again as he heard her go past, though she *crept* in the hope he was asleep. She threw the armful of clothes into the bath, tamped them down with the bath-brush till the suds covered them, and then went to pick up Darren and carry him down. Colleen had nearly reached the bottom step by the time Maura got to the top.

"You're slow as a fast-day," Maura said cheerfully as she pushed past with Darren over her shoulder.

Coll made better time on the flat than on the stairs and they reached the kitchen together. Their mother was still outside hunting for Foley. The strange girl sat where Maura had left her. Her face was pink and puzzled. She was chewing and chewing. But to Maura's astonishment, no more squares of bread were missing from her plate.

"Don't tell me you're still chewing away on your first bit!" she exclaimed. The girl nodded anxiously. "Swallow it now! Oh, come on—let it slip til' the back of your throat and then go like this—" She did an exaggerated swallow.

After a few seconds of frowning concentration, the girl did the same. A smile of relief spread over her face and she reached for another square of bread. This time there was no problem. She chewed, swallowed with a loud gulp, and popped in the next bit.

"This one is different!" she announced.

"That was a plain one, with no marmalade. Not so good."

"It *is* good, it's *good*," said the girl with her mouth full.

Maura watched her curiously. One would think she'd never eaten anything before. Then she shrugged and turned to the cooker. The bacon was just right; she dished it onto the plates and broke three eggs into the hot bacon-fat.

Colleen's little squares of bread and marmalade had disappeared rapidly, with quite a lot of the marmalade getting onto her fingers and face. As she munched, she stared at the girl. Maura was a bit worried—Coll didn't like strangers. But evidently she didn't mind this one. She suddenly reached out a sticky hand and stroked the girl's bright brown curls.

"Mor," she said discoveringly. That was the best she could do about Maura's name. Then she pointed to Maura and said, "Mor" again. "Mor-Mor," she concluded, and burst out laughing with her mouth full.

Maura leaned towards the other girl. "Sorry about her manners," she whispered. "I told you. She's not-bright."

"Not-bright?"

"In the head."

"She is bright in the soul," said the girl, very matter-of-factly.

And suddenly when she said that, something quite extraordinary happened.

Colleen, still stroking the girl's hair with marmalady fingers, began to sing. Nothing unusual about that. The incredible thing was what and *how* she sang.

> *"Alling by un boooofinul, all keetern day un Ma—*
> *Alling why un waaaaanerful, an ol' Go' made un aw!"*

Anyone who didn't know Colleen wouldn't have been able to make anything out of the words. But Maura knew Colleen very well indeed. She had been listening to her speech since babyhood, and never had she heard her say or sing anything even half so clearly.

As to the tune—well, Colleen wasn't so bad with tunes, you could often tell what she was trying to sing, but this time nearly all the notes were right. It was as clear as clear what she was singing: the very same hymn that Maura had already heard twice that day—once in assembly and once when the girl began singing in the street where the bomb had gone off.

Maura sat at the tea-table, stunned. She was staring at Colleen, singing away at the top of her voice, her bulgy eyes on the girl's face, her fingers now clutching her hair. She must have been hurting, but the girl didn't move. She just looked at Colleen. Such a funny look! Gentle. *Loving*. How could you possibly love Colleen unless you knew her? Even then it was hard sometimes—Maura certainly couldn't love Colleen when she was pulling her hair.

What's happening? she thought to herself.

She didn't say it aloud, but the girl turned her head towards her just as if she'd heard the question, and smiled a strange, sweet, perfect smile.

Maura's insides seemed to turn to water and everything around her, all the solid everyday things, rushed away in every direction until there was nothing to be seen but the girl's beautiful face, shining in the midst of a sort of daylight darkness. It wasn't just a "shining face" as one might say about a face that was clean or cheerful. The light actually seemed to radiate from her skin, from her eyes and even her hair.

Maura had a strong impulse to fall onto her knees,

but she didn't, chiefly because they felt like jelly. She was afraid to move at all in case she just melted into the floor. It was the strangest feeling she had ever felt. As if she had no body.

Then, suddenly, the back door banged back against the wall and her mother came stamping in, herding Foley in front of her, scolding him loudly for making her look for him. The noise did worse than startle Maura; it shocked her, like a blow. She put both hands to her head as if she'd been woken from a deep, deep sleep.

"Good heavens, Maura! How can you sit there looking at your sister pulling at that poor child's hair? Colleen, let go, you'll hurt her, so you will!"

Ma hurried forward and forcefully loosened Coll's gripping fingers and wiped them briskly with a wet cloth.

"Foley, eat your dinner. No, wait! Wash your hands first. How often do you have to be told? Oh, you need your daddy, so you do! And just look at these eggs now, cooked to rubber! How I'm supposed to do everything and look after everything on my own, I do not know . . ." She paused, her eyes on the girl. "What a shame, your lovely hair's all matted and sticky!" Her strident voice stopped and her work-thickened fingers played, as if by their own will, through that lovely shiny hair.

Surely she can *see!* thought Maura, staring and staring.

After stroking for a moment, Maura's mother bent and looked into the girl's face.

"What's your name, darlin'?"

"Angela," said the girl at once.

Maura had no time to digest her own surprise at this. She thought her mother was going to faint. She staggered, putting her hand out to stop herself from falling, and clutching Colleen's solid shoulder.

"It can't be!" she whispered. "Angela! But that was *her* name."

"Whose name, Ma?" cried Maura, glad to find she could speak, and that all the things in the kitchen had come back into their normal places.

When her mother didn't answer, but only stood there, white and weak-looking, Maura turned on the girl. The feelings she had had a moment or two before had faded like a dream—she could hardly remember them somehow. Now the girl was just a girl, sitting there in Maura's old raincoat with jam in her hair. And she'd been fooling her, evidently.

"You told me you didn't know your name!" she said accusingly.

The girl said, "When your mother asked me, I remembered it."

"Oh, sure! I bet you knew it all the time." Maura felt unaccountably upset. She got up from the table and began automatically stacking the plates and carrying them to the sink. She was afraid she was stupidly going to start crying and she felt desperately tired.

Five

COLLEEN WAS QUITE exceptionally good that evening. She sat in front of the television, singing away to herself, rocking contentedly from side to side; and when it was time for her bed she didn't protest at all, but went as nicely as you please, beaming and humming around at them all. She even waved to Angela, who was sitting watching television too, with Foley curled up on the old sofa beside her.

Maura was not in such a happy mood as the others. The most awful thing had happened. She realized it only when she went upstairs, after washing-up the tea things, to get started on her homework.

She'd left her bags—both of them, books *and* sports things—lying on the pavement near where she'd fallen. *Miles* away.

When she first thought of it, she'd been on the landing upstairs. She'd stopped cold, her mind in an uproar. All her books! All her pencils and pens, her math set that her da had bought her—her school library book, everything! She'd be killed, just killed, at school, never mind what her mother would have to say.

Maura was no cry-baby, but the tears which it suddenly seemed she had been fighting off ever since the bomb, now burst out of her eyes, and she leaned against the scuffed wall-paper under the picture of the Sacred Heart and wept into her sleeve.

She heard swift, light footsteps running up the stairs and tried to duck into her bedroom, but Angela was beside her before she could move.

"Maura?"

"What," said Maura with a deep sniff.

"What are you doing?"

"Girnin'. What does it look like?" said Maura ungraciously.

"Girnin'?" asked Angela, in that funny, puzzled way, as if she'd never heard the word.

Maura was in no mood to be patient. She turned to face Angela and, with a finger in each eye, smeared the ready tears roughly down her cheeks.

"Yes, girnin'! Crying! Tears, look! Haven't you ever seen a wee tear before?" Angela was looking at her in the strangest way, her eyes full of something more than pity, a sort of horror. "You can call me cry-baby if you like," hissed Maura fiercely. "You'd cry, same as me, if you'd lost all your books *and* your sports things. And it's all your fault, so it is, now I think of it!"

"My—fault?" whispered Angela in a tone that matched her look. "Those—" she pointed to the tears, and then snatched her hand away as if they had burned her fingertips—"Those are because of *me?*"

Maura was startled by her horrified tone.

"Oh, come on, it's not *so* bad." She gave herself a shake and went into the bathroom to get some toilet paper to blow her nose. Angela followed. "It's only that if it hadn't been for you, I mightn't have forgotten them."

She blew her nose fiercely several times, flushed the paper away and washed her face. When she looked around, Angela was standing perfectly still just behind her.

She was not wearing Maura's raincoat any more. Straight after tea, before the dishes, Maura had brought her upstairs and given her a pair of her old jeans and a gray school sweater of the kind that might have been anybody's—she didn't think her mother would notice that they were Maura's own. Angela looked more—more *ordinary* in these than in the coat, and so Maura felt more comfortable with her.

But now she stood there with her head thrown back, her eyes tightly closed and her thin arms, in the gray wool sweater, stiff at her sides. She looked very dramatic, and Maura, who had no patience for anything exaggerated, gave her a little shake.

"Oh, get away, stop that. I don't really blame you! I should have remembered . . . Anyway, it's too late now. And at least it means no homework . . . Let's go down and watch telly."

So that's what they'd done, all of them, even Darren, who sat on his mother's knee and stared, not at the lighted screen but at Angela. He cooed and stretched his fat hands toward her. After a bit, Ma got up to go and make some tea and dumped him on Angela's knee.

Maura thought, Oh-oh, now look out for trouble! Foley, an unusually silent child, especially since Kieran and Da went, could lose his temper quick enough if he were displeased, and Maura could see that he had "taken over" Angela and wanted her to himself. His face puckered into a scowl. He jerked away from Angela's side and opened his mouth, but when she smiled and put her arm around him, the scowl simply slid off his face, and he nestled at her side again. He even let Darren bang him on the head with his fist.

What with Colleen good as gold, and Ma slicing currant-bread, Maura couldn't remember when things had been so peaceful and nice. If only she didn't have to worry about her lost books!

After the tea, Ma went upstairs to see to Colleen and Maura took Darren to bed, leaving Foley and Angela still cuddled up in front of the telly. Normally Ma would have insisted on Maura coping with Colleen while she put Darren down (a much easier job), but tonight she said, "You leave Coll to me, darlin'. I can see you're all done up." Ma must've been done up too, after her shift at the mill, but Maura really did feel extra tired tonight so she didn't say anything. Just tumbled the sleepy Darren into his cot, blew on his tum a couple of times, pulled the old blanket up on him, closed the cot-side and tiptoed out, thankful that he didn't yell for her to come back as usual.

That was when the doorbell rang.

It was only eight o'clock but everyone in the house stopped whatever they were doing and looked fearfully at whoever was nearest. Even Colleen, who sensed things without knowing, started to whimper. Ma soothed her briefly, then hurried downstairs, taking off her apron. "It's not the soldiers," she muttered to Maura as she passed, "not their knock. And if it's the Provos, who else can they take? Foley?" Maura was thinking it might be her da, or news of him, but then if so they'd likely come around to the back in case a British patrol happened to be passing.

She peered over the bannister into the little hall. Ma opened the door cautiously after putting the chain on.

"What are you wantin'?" she asked suspiciously.

Maura heard an indistinct voice outside, a man's voice. Then Ma shut the door, undid the chain, and opened it again.

The next thing Maura saw made her fairly gape.

Her bags—both of them—were being passed in by a shadowy figure outside.

Ma was saying thank you in a bewildered way. Then she closed the door and looked around and up at Maura on the stairs.

"What have you got to say about these?" she asked severely, dangling the bags, or rather shaking them at Maura with a stern look.

Maura rushed down the remaining stairs and grabbed them in incredulous delight. "My bags! I left them there, on the ground, near where the bomb was! Who was that man, Ma? Why did he bring them?"

"He said he found them and brought them to you. Said he thought you might be needing them to do your homework."

Maura was clasping the bags joyfully to her chest. "But how did he know?"

"What?"

"Where I live!"

"From your books, of course! Just as well you finally wrote your name and address in all your books, like you've been told to a hundred times."

Maura stared at her. "Yes," she said at last, "just as well."

She carried her restored treasures upstairs. Colleen was already asleep—she fell asleep the minute her head touched the pillow. So Maura switched on her little desk light and opened the schoolbag and tipped everything it contained onto her desk. Then she went through the books, one by one. Was it possible she had written her address in one of them without remembering it? If so, she couldn't find it. The thing was a total mystery.

She pushed it from her mind. It was a technique she had mastered long ago. She sat down at her desk and began—as a sort of penance—with math. Tired as she was, it went better than usual—not easily, but better. One or two of the sums seemed to do themselves. Maybe she was catching on at last? History next. Not too bad. Then R. K.

When she looked up at last, Angela was standing beside her.

"I thought you had lost your books."

Maura beamed up at her. "Would you believe it? Some lovely man brought my things back!"

"Oh."

"You don't realize! It's like a holy miracle. It's fantastic enough he bothered. All that way! But how did he know where to come? I just can't get over it—"

While she chattered on, Angela was slowly picking up the books and looking at them. She dropped the first one, as if taken by surprise at its weight. She turned them over and looked inside them and stroked their pages. Maura was startled to see her bend and rub her lips across the lines of dull print.

"I wouldn't do that! They're not so very clean," she said. "Maeve O'Neill had that before me, and she had *nits*." And then she was silent.

Turning the pages, backwards, Angela had come to the front inside cover. And there, written in the most *exquisite* writing Maura had ever seen in her life, even finer and with more little curlicues than Sister Josephine's, she read:

Maura Cuddy,
23 Rider Street,
W. Belfast.

Six

Maura lay in bed that night and thought.

Her mother had not behaved in any way as Maura expected. She hadn't done a *thing* about finding out who Angela was, or phoning the police, or anything. She seemed just to take it for granted that Angela would stay the night with them, and had made the sleeping arrangements in her briskest and most no-nonsense way.

"Foley can sleep with Colleen tonight, and you can go into Foley's wee bed, Maura. Angela will have Kieran's bed."

Kieran's bed! Foley was forbidden even to sit on Kieran's bed! But at least it was ready. It had clean, ironed sheets on it and the best quilt and the last of the down pillows from Ma's "bottom drawer," her collection of linen that she'd made for her wedding, twenty-two years ago.

"And don't forget your prayers," Ma called after them as they went up to bed. "You've more than usual to be thankful for tonight!"

So for once in her life, Maura wasn't lying listening to Colleen's loud, contented snores. Foley was. Maura was in Foley's bed, listening to Angela's gentle breathing; and after a long time she thought, That's not how people breathe when they're asleep. And she whispered, "Angela!"

"Yes?" came Angela's voice in the dark.

It was such a pretty voice. It sounded terribly sleepy, though.

"Can you not go to sleep?"

There was a silence, and then Angela said, with a little plea in her voice, "How?"

Maura sat up and looked across at Angela, lying there under Kieran's revolutionary-hero posters. Was there a glow about her face, or was it just her paleness in the street-light? Her eyes were wide open, anyway.

"Angela, do you not know—*anything?*" Maura whispered. But she wasn't impatient or sarcastic now, just curious and a bit pitying.

"I learn quickly when you tell me. Don't I?"

"Sure you do . . ." Maura hesitated, then crept out of bed and took the two steps that separated hers from Angela's. "Now. First, turn over on your side. That's better. I can never fall asleep on my back. Put your hand under your cheek. Draw up your knees. Are you comfortable?"

"Yes . . ."

"Close your eyes, then. Relax. Think of nice things."

After a moment, Angela said, "I can't."

"Why not?"

"I can only think of—of the bomb. The fire. Those people!"

She shuddered and suddenly turned her face into Kieran's soft pillow and then she began to tremble and her thin little shoulders, under Maura's nightie, began to heave. And Maura knew she was crying, or trying not to cry—or trying *to* cry, for the thing and the people they had seen that afternoon.

Maura sat on the mat beside the bed and gently stroked her friend's hair. "Just—sort of—let yourself go," she advised. She frowned, thinking about *how* one cried. "Big gulps of air—that's right—let it out— you'll feel much better. Oh, that was a good one!" she exclaimed, as a great sob shook Angela and a muffled groan came out of the pillow. And soon tears were flowing freely. Almost too much so! Angela cried on and on, heartbrokenly. Maura sat by her and patted her back and made soothing noises, the way she did with Colleen or Foley, or Darren, though none of them ever cried like that.

At last, after a long time, it stopped. Angela's wet face became peaceful and her eyes closed and her breathing grew regular. Her white hand lay open like a water-lily on the pillow.

Maura felt so sorry for her! She didn't know how it could be that anyone who had lived to be eleven years old in this city could still be so sensitive about the Troubles, and she certainly didn't know how anyone could live even half that long, anywhere, and not know how to walk or run or eat or cry or fall asleep. But she was sorry for her. And something more than that, something that made her, after she'd stood up, lean over Angela's sleeping form and pop a quick kiss on her wet, white cheek.

Something happened to her lips. It was like a magic whiteness that spread from them all over her body. She stood still and straight, touching them with her fingers. The feeling flowed all through her. She waited, unable to move, until it reached her toes and her fingertips and her eyebrows and her hair-roots and then died away.

Maura went back slowly to Foley's bed and knelt down beside it and stayed there until she fell asleep, which wasn't long. She couldn't think of a single prayer to say but it didn't matter. She didn't want to pray, she just wanted to kneel there and feel happy.

When she woke up in the morning, she was safe in bed, not on the floor at all. She had no idea how she'd got there. Perhaps she'd crawled in, in her sleep. Anyway she'd had a wonderful rest, a deep, deep sleep without dreams. She felt as if she'd slept for a week.

She jumped up and ran over to look at Angela. She was still sleeping soundly. Maybe if she didn't know how to fall asleep, she would need help waking up, too! Maura gave her a little shake.

"Angela! Wake up. It's morning."

Angela half opened her eyes and rolled over on her back. Her pale face was rosier now, and her eyes were a little bit bunged-up like ordinary eyes. She even had sleepy-dust. She smiled at Maura—actually it was more of a grin.

"I love sleeping! I don't want to wake up yet."

"Lazybones! I've got jobs before school. You come on and help."

Maura dressed quickly. Her school blouse had got dirty when she fell the day before and she had no spare, so she fished out one of Patrick's shirts. At first, after Pat died, she hadn't even looked at any of his things, but now she didn't mind. She even liked to wear his clothes, it made her feel a bit close to him. She was looking at herself in her mirror while she tied her tie, when Angela's face appeared over her shoulder.

"That's Patrick's clothe, isn't it?" she said, touching the shirt.

Maura froze, but only for a moment. How did she know about Pat . . . ? But these strange flashes of knowledge didn't frighten Maura today as they had yesterday.

"Yes," she said. "Only you shouldn't say 'clothe.' You can't have *one* of clothes."

"Do I talk all right usually?" asked Angela anxiously.

Maura nodded. "Not bad," she said. She was trying to curl her hair around her finger to make it more like Angela's. "How d'you get your hair to go in curls like that?" she asked.

"I don't know. Show me how to use that," she said, pointing to the comb.

Maura showed her, and soon she could do it herself quite well. Maura stood watching, marveling at how beautiful she was, but how un—un—un*used*.

"How did you bear it?"

"What?" asked Maura, startled.

"When Patrick—you know."

"Well. It was awful. Not just him dying but how much he hurt. They couldn't give him anything much for the pain because . . . Oh, I don't know why, but they had reasons." She hesitated, and then confessed something she'd never told anyone except the priest. "At first when he died I was glad."

Angela turned swiftly. "Ah! Because he was going to heaven?"

"No. Because he stopped hurting. Because he stopped yelling. Because he stopped hurting *me*."

Angela stared at her.

"I don't understand," she said slowly.

"No, I don't suppose you do."

There was a silence between them. They didn't do anything, they just stood there feeling like strangers, as if there were a great gulf between them. Maura felt she couldn't stand it. She'd thought Angela was going to be her best friend, and now there she was, looking at her as if she were infectious.

"There's such an awful lot to learn," said Angela helplessly at last.

"About what?"

Angela shook her head and spread out her hands.

"About—about—*why*," she said.

Maura was still feeling bristly.

"Why what? What're you talking about?"

"Don't be angry with me. *Please!*"

"Then don't be looking at me like that, all disgusted."

"I wasn't!"

"Yes, you were so."

"No! No! Don't you see? I don't know about—hurting. I don't know how it makes you feel. I have to find out *why* you were glad when Patrick died."

Slowly, Maura turned away to make the bed. Angela, watching over her shoulder, copied her.

"Why—*what?*" Maura asked after a bit.

"For instance, yesterday."

"Why do they put bombs, d'you mean?"

Angela nodded.

Maura shrugged and moved over to finish off Angela's bed which, despite her best efforts, was still all rumply.

"Don't ask me. It's to do with religion."

"Religion?"

"Well, in a way," said Maura hastily. It seemed wrong to link bomb-planting with God. "I mean, it's the Catholics against the Protestants, the IRA against the UDA, the Provos against the UVF, and the English soldiers getting in the middle and messing things up more. Now the INLAs have split from the Provos and the Protestants murder each other too sometimes . . . it's all mixed up."

Angela was sitting on the bed listening intently,

but looking utterly bewildered, as well she might, Maura thought.

"It's been going on for ages. Hundred of years, Da says. You can't learn all about it in five minutes."

"Do *you* understand it?"

"N-no. Not really. Girls don't bother about it much. It's men's business. Here, put some clothes on."

"Can I go to school in these?" Angela pointed to the jeans.

"Oh! Are you after coming to school with me?"

"I want to do everything you do."

"I don't know what Sister Josephine's going to say about that!" But Maura's heart lightened. *She* wanted Angela to do everything with her, too. "I'll lend you a wee skirt for school. Do you know how to wash your face and clean your teeth?"

Angela didn't. And there was something else she didn't know either, and *that* Maura had a hard time teaching her because she was too shy. But in the end nature took over, and Angela came out of the bathroom laughing and saying it "felt nice," almost as nice as eating and sleeping. Maura had never thought of it like that, but when Angela said it, she realized it was true.

While they were going down to breakfast, Maura had a funny thought. What might it feel like if you did all these things for the *very first time* when you were her age, instead of having done them always, from when you were a baby, and got so used to all the sensations that you hardly noticed them any more? It was fun to think about, and somehow it helped her to understand Angela better.

Seven

BREAKFAST WAS SPECIAL that morning. Whether because Angela was staying or "just because," Ma had been out early and bought one of those Kellogg's packets with all the different little boxes of cereals so they could each pick what they wanted.

Of course Foley would have to want the same one Maura did, the Cocopops, but it wouldn't do to have a row in front of Angela, so Maura gave way and had the plain cornflakes. She was very puzzled to find that they tasted chocolaty. Maybe it was because her mouth had been watering for the Cocopops and her imagination was doing her a favor.

Foley, meanwhile, was so surprised she'd given in to him that he let Colleen have a couple of big spoonsful of his to taste. This proved to be a mistake. She started kicking up a terrific shindy then, wanting to have the rest, shouting and banging her spoon and trying to drag Foley's bowl towards her, and all might have ended in chaos and disaster, as so many meals with Colleen did.

But Angela, who had been tucking into her Rice Krispies with an expression of absolute bliss on her face, concentrating on crunching them between her teeth, swiftly put a spoonful of those into Colleen's open mouth.

The whole family gasped with dismay. Pop something into Colleen's mouth when she was shouting and she'd be liable to blow it right back in your eye, or choke. But not this time. A look of delight came over her usually rather blank face. She closed her mouth and chewed and chewed with her eyes half-shut like a cow chewing the cud. Then she swallowed, opened eyes and mouth wide and turned to Angela for more.

"Just look at that, will you?" said Ma, laughing. "Like a wee cuckoo in the nest!" And Colleen, crunching, laughed too, giving Angela a milk-spray, but she didn't seem to mind.

After breakfast Maura showed Angela how to wash up. Oddly enough, she found this boring task the greatest fun. It wasn't so much getting the plates clean, as watching how the water ran off them and fell onto the draining-board and from there into the sink.

"Why does it go down and not fly up?" Angela asked.

"It just does," said Maura. "Everything does."

"Gravity," said her mother briefly. She was feeding Darren in his high chair.

"Oh, yes!" said Maura, remembering. "It's a law."

"A law . . ." said Angela thoughtfully, holding a cup up to watch it drip. "There must be a lot and a lot of these laws."

"Well . . . that's one kind." There was the other kind, too, with police and judges and prisons, but Maura didn't feel like bringing all that up. But her mother seemed to be following her thoughts.

"Speaking of laws," she said with a sudden rough edge to her voice (which had been noticeably softer this morning than usual), "tomorrow's visiting day." She picked Darren up, put him in his pram and wheeled him out into the yard, kicking the door shut behind her with a bang that made Angela jump.

"Oh—!" she gasped, putting her fingers to her ears.

"It's only Ma slamming the door, she always does it."

"Noises hurt me."

"Your ears?"

"All over."

"You'll have to get over *that*, so you will," said Maura briskly, collecting Darren's dishes. "There's not much quiet in Belfast. C'mon, finish up now, or we'll miss the bus til' school." She was thinking of yesterday. It was so much easier when Ma was up and about, and Maura didn't have to rush around like a maddy, trying to do everything and still going off to school with a bad conscience.

On the bus, Angela asked, "What did your mother mean when she said, 'Tomorrow's visiting day'?"

"Oh, that . . ." Maura turned her face away. "My brother Kieran's in the Maze."

"What's the Maze?"

Maura looked around at her unbelievingly. However ignorant you were, how could you not have heard of the Maze? But then she remembered that Angela didn't know anything. Even that.

"Sure it's the big prison," she said, keeping her voice low so the others in the bus couldn't hear.

"Prison." Angela closed her eyes and sat for a moment with her head bent as if thinking. "That's a place where people are shut away when they've . . . committed . . . sins," she said with a little frown, as if not sure if she'd got it right.

"I wouldn't say *that*. Sure if they put you in prison for every little sin there'd be nobody outside! It's for criminals. Mainly."

"And so your brother is a—?"

"No! He's not. Not a regular one. He's a political, even if they won't give him status."

Angela closed her eyes again. Maura had the notion that when she did that, it was like going to the library or looking something up in a dictionary, but perhaps that was silly. Anyway, it didn't work this time. Angela looked up after a minute and shook her head.

"Being a political means you're in prison for doing something to help the Provos. The IRA," she added, now in a whisper. "What's that?"

It was Maura's turn now to scowl and shut her eyes, trying to remember what Kieran and her da had told her.

"It's a—well, it's an organization. A group of men. They're wanting us to unite with the Republic. That's the other part of Ireland. They want us all to be Catholics and to get rid of the British. Or something like that."

"And what sins do they commit to get put in prison for?"

"They're not sinners at all, so they're not! How could they be, when they're all good Catholics?"

"Are Catholics people who never sin?"

"I never said that. Everyone sins sometimes. But it's no sin to fight for your country."

"Is Kieran a soldier?"

"He was one, till they caught him."

"Who did he fight?"

"Different people."

"The British?"

"Them too. He hated them."

"Why? What did they do to him?"

"When he was only fourteen an English soldier hit him with his rifle."

"Why?"

"For nothing. Because he's a Catholic."

"Hadn't he done *anything* to the soldier?"

"He might have thrown a wee stone. Sure, a lot of the boys do that. The soldier didn't have to knock his teeth out. Da took him to court and we got three hundred pounds. He said he lost his temper."

"Who did?"

"The *soldier*," said Maura. "But Kieran swore he'd get even. I thought he'd forget about it after he got his new teeth. I mean, they were real good teeth, straighter than the old ones. But when he left school and couldn't get work and was on the 'buru—' "

"What's the buru?"

"The Bureau. Gettin' money from the government instead of a job. He was hanging around with a lot of other boys and he couldn't stick it. It's not the same for boys. I mean if I don't get a job I shan't mind, I'll have the housework to do, and the shopping and all that, but the lads haven't a thing to pass the time except drinking and goin' til' the Youth Center."

"Is it fun there?"

"*I* like it well enough, but for big boys it's no use."

"So he became a soldier."

"Not a real one with a uniform. A secret one. He joined the Provos. Like Da did later. And we didn't see much of him because he went across the water—"

"To England?"

"Yes. Then he came back for a while, and then he went off again, and next thing he was arrested." She was talking very quietly now.

"Had he done anything really—bad?" asked Angela.

"Listen, he was fighting the enemy! If it weren't for the likes of him, they'd start burning our houses down again, like they used to!"

"The British burned down your houses?"

"*No*, silly, the Unionists did it, but the Brits weren't much help, were they?"

"Why? Why?"

"I don't know. I wish you'd stop asking so many questions."

There was silence for a while. The bus was driving past a British police-post, going very slowly over the road-ramps.

"I love the bumps," remarked Angela. "Flying is so *smooth.*" She said "smooth" as if she meant "boring."

"You've been in an airplane?" asked Maura enviously.

"No," said Angela, puzzled. And then she pointed. "Look! There's a poem. On the wall." She read it aloud.

"Oh soldier boy, why did you come
With your hatred and your gun?
Our land was good and green with grass,
We were happy till you stole our laugh.
You ruined our home, you destroyed our past,
I tell you now, soldier, your presence won't last."

She had forgotten to whisper. A man sitting in front turned around and growled angrily, "Shut up, you'd better, you big-mouthed wee betch!"

Angela's fingers flew to her ears. Maura blushed scarlet. At that moment the bus turned into the main street where the bomb had gone off the day before, and all the passengers began pointing and exclaiming. It was time for the girls to get off, and as they did they craned their necks like the others to look at the scene of the explosion.

Traffic was normal again, and you couldn't see much—they'd boarded up the café and even stood the bus-stop up again, though it looked pretty knocked about. Maura touched it as she passed, feeling sorry for it. Angela turned her head away, and Maura had to stop her walking in the road to keep as far as possible from the front of the bombed café.

When they arrived at school and walked through the yard, Maura noticed some other girls staring. She held Angela's hand and led her through the front hall to Sister Josephine's outer office. The secretary looked put out.

"You can't just be bringing all your friends and relations into school without a by-your-leave, Maura!" she said sharply. "What a notion!"

"But I can't leave her outside," said Maura. "She wants to be with me, and she wants to go to school. Don't you, Angela?" Angela nodded eagerly, but the secretary, a plain, vinegary-faced woman who never smiled, was unmoved.

"I'll ask Sister Josephine," she said thinly, "but I can tell you the answer will be no." And she stamped on her bony legs into the inner office.

Angela sat on the bench and swung her feet. She was wearing rather grubby long, white socks and a pair of Maura's lace-ups, her new ones, while Maura wore an old, old pair that should have been thrown away. Lucky she'd kept them. Maura was worried, but Angela wasn't. She threw Maura a smile as if to say, "It'll be okay."

And it was. Sister Josephine put a cross face around her door, as if just ready to say, No. But when she caught sight of Angela, her face changed. The rest of her, in her gray habit, followed her head into the secretary's office.

"What's your name, dear?"

"Angela."

"Stand up, Angela, when you talk to me." But she said it very nicely. Angela stood up. Sister Josephine looked at her. It was amazing, thought Maura, how her shabby, scruffy old clothes suddenly looked almost new. Even the grayish socks shone white, and the shoes gleamed, though Maura hadn't polished them for over a week.

"Well, I must say," said Sister Josephine, "your cousin does credit to the school uniform. More than you do, Maura." Maura made a face behind her back and nearly made Angela giggle. "How long will she be staying with you?"

"I don't know," said Maura, somehow startled by the question.

"I suppose we could stretch a point, if it's not for too long," said Sister Josephine, much to the secretary's disgust. "Just take her into your class with you, Maura, and give her some help if she needs it. Make sure nobody teases her. What about her lunch?"

"Sandwiches," said Maura.

"All right then, off you go."

As they turned to leave, Sister Josephine patted Angela on the shoulder. Maura saw a funny look pass over her face. She stood there quite still, looking at her hand as if it had just given her a lovely surprise.

Maura had the best day at school she could ever remember.

To begin with, far from teasing, the other girls made a beeline for Angela and treated her as if she were the best friend of all of them. All Maura had to do was stop them half pulling her to pieces, between wanting to touch her hair and stroke her arms and hands and make her say things so they could marvel at her strange, tinkly voice.

"What kind of an accent is that?" asked their English teacher when she had asked Angela a question, to draw her into the lesson, and she had said sweetly, "I don't know." Now she said it again.

"But I mean, where do you come from?"

"From up there," said Angela. And pointed upward.

There was a paralyzed silence in the room, the kind of silence that comes before hoots of laughter. Maura grew tense, waiting. But the teacher, even though she was not a nun, said quite quietly, "Well, I suppose we might all say that," and the laugh just fluttered out harmlessly. "I meant, what country do you come from? You're not from Ireland, are you?"

Maura was suddenly frightened. If Angela said, "I don't know," to a question like that, people might begin to suspect she was . . . Well. It mustn't be allowed to happen.

"She comes from up—north!" she said. "Far up

north, as far as you can get. They . . . they don't have any accent, you know, up—there."

"Is that a fact," said the teacher. She gave her a funny look, but she went on with the lesson.

Apart from that, everything went well. Unnaturally well, Maura couldn't help feeling. Even the math class was fun, because, quite suddenly, she found she understood base 3 and long division, both of which had totally eluded her until now. It was such a relief! Like a curtain opening and letting in the sun and showing a rather exciting view with lots going on in it. She sat there doing sums one after the other as easily as falling off a log. Oh, if only she didn't forget by next lesson!

In her not-so-bad lessons, like geography, history and R.K., the teachers just kept asking things she knew, *and* picking on hers out of the little forest of hands to answer them. And the way the words flowed out of her! She'd never been able to think or talk like that before.

It was like when the new supermarket had opened in town—Maura and Foley had marched through the glass doors and wandered around among all the new shelves and counters and freezer-boxes looking at the thousands of lovely things there were to buy. All you needed was some money; but in a way it didn't matter. What mattered was it was all there, *available*, when and if you ever could afford to pay for it.

Maura never bothered envying rich people. She liked their being there, because if they weren't, how could you dream of being rich one day yourself? It was like that with the supermarket and it was like that with the lovely thing that happened that school day in her head. Shelves and counters and baskets of possibilities in there, just waiting till she had earned enough to buy them and bring them out. What she produced that day in lessons was like a free sample.

And all the homework she had done the night before was right.

Eight

As a thank-offering for getting her books back, Maura sat for ten minutes at break in a corner of the yard and copied her name and address into every textbook and notebook.

When she'd finished, she looked around for Angela. She was not hard to spot. The big crowd of children in one corner of the playground must have her in the middle. Again, Maura felt that little stab of jealousy. Angela was *her* friend! And no sooner had she thought this than she saw Angela pushing out through the crowd and running toward her.

How much she'd learned since yesterday! Now she not only ran well, she hardly seemed to touch the ground—she skimmed. In a few seconds, it seemed, she was at Maura's side, a little breathless, saying, "Don't, Maura. I'm *your* friend!" like an echo of Maura's jealous thought.

Maura hung her head. "How did you know what I was thinking?"

"I don't know," said Angela as usual.

But she was saying it less and less as the day went by.

After lunch it was games. They played netball. Maura had brought an extra pair of shorts and a T-shirt for Angela. After the first few minutes of standing and watching, Angela went up to the teacher.

"May I play?" she asked.

"I thought you said you didn't know the game," said the games teacher acidly.

"I'd like to try," said Angela.

She was put on the reserve bench. Maura saw her sitting there, watching longingly, so she pretended she'd twisted her ankle.

Angela began to play center. When the ball was thrown up, she leaped into the air and although she only seemed to tap the ball, it flew right down the pitch to the basket area. There it was caught and flipped in before the other team knew what had happened. Later, Angela scored five baskets herself. Every time she tried for one, she got it in. Both teams were roaring.

"What is she, some kind of miracle-worker?" one of the opposing team was heard to ask bitterly. The teacher took Maura aside. "Your cousin told me she'd never played. What a tarradiddle! Never mind. She'd be quite an asset to the school team! Is she staying long?"

Maura was nearly bursting with pride.

But the beaten team had no reason to feel so warmly toward Angela. As they all ran back to the huts to change, there was a sudden cry. Maura looked around to see Angela lying flat on the tarmac.

Everyone crowded around her as she sat up.

"Are you hurt?" asked Maura anxiously.

"No, I don't think so," said Angela. But when she stood up they all saw blood oozing from her knee.

"Into Mrs. Driscoll's room and have it seen to," said the teacher. "Maura, go with her."

As they walked along the corridor, Angela began to limp.

"What happened?" asked Maura. "Did you just fall?"

"That tall girl put her foot in front of me," said Angela with a puzzled expression.

Maura's eyes narrowed and she pursed her lips. "That's Eileen O'Malley all over! Just 'cause you beat her! I'll kill her, so I will!"

Angela stopped in her tracks. "Maura!" she cried, her face full of horror.

"Oh, I don't mean kill her to *death*. But I'll get back at her just the same."

"You mustn't!"

"You don't know her. She's horrible."

"But you're not!"

Maura didn't want to continue the conversation. She piloted Angela firmly to Mrs. Driscoll, who sat her on a bench and washed the cut.

"What a shame, on that lovely white skin . . . How have you reached your age without a few knee-scars?

Well, you've got one now, I'm afraid . . . This may hurt a bit," she added, pouring something sinister out of a bottle onto some cotton wool. "Must get all the germs out, mustn't we?"

The next minute Angela was screaming blue murder.

Maura had never heard anyone make such a noise about a hurt since Patrick. The screams reminded her so much of him, of that awful time, that she felt she couldn't stand it. She rushed over to Angela and grabbed her arm quite roughly.

"Shut up, will you, shut up!" she cried furiously. "It's nothing but a wee sting!"

Mrs. Driscoll, who had been about to say the same thing (without the "shut-ups"), said instead, "Now, Maura, we must try to be more sympathetic. Some people have a lower pain-threshold than others." She pressed a dressing over Angela's knee with a practiced hand. "There! Isn't that better? What a noise! Ts, ts! One would think you'd never felt a little pain before."

Maura helped Angela, who was now white but silent, out of the room. Maura was upset and shaking.

"Whatever got into you? It can't have been as bad as all that!"

Angela looked at her blankly. "What was it?"

"What?"

"That terrible—awful—thing. In my knee."

"I tell you it was *nothing at all*. Nothing but a wee pain."

"You've—felt—that?"

"Thousands and thousands of times," said Maura. "D'you want to see *my* knees?" And she showed them, covered with little white scars and two big new bruises from yesterday.

Angela stared at them.

"I don't understand," she said slowly. "That—pain—that I felt—that's something *usual?*"

Maura was still upset, and being upset made her sharp-tongued.

"Are you mad? It's going on all the time, from when you're a baby. When Darren bumps his *head* he doesn't make such a fuss! When Foley fell off the wall and *broke his wrist*, he didn't! How do you think you'll manage when you're really hurt?"

Angela was silent. She limped back to class.

Luckily the next lesson was science. Almost from the start, Angela was fascinated. She followed the teacher around the classroom like a little dog, watching everything with such intense interest that the others began to laugh at her, but she didn't care. While the others were checking homework, the teacher let her walk about looking at the aquarium and the charts and the jars with beans growing, and the white mice.

"It's wonderful, wonderful!" she kept whispering to Maura. She seemed to have forgotten all about her knee.

Since they were soon going up to the secondary school where there'd be a proper laboratory, the teacher had brought in some scientific apparatus, and used it to show them a real experiment.

It was quite complicated; Maura couldn't remember beyond step 2 when it came to writing it down. But Angela put her hand up. "Can I do it?" she asked eagerly.

"You want to repeat the experiment?" asked the teacher in surprise. "All right, come along and try."

And Angela did it. She did it exactly as the teacher had, only more quickly. Her fingers seemed to have a life of their own, and the apparatus behaved as if it were alive too, doing her orders. Maura, watching, marveled that only yesterday she had thought Angela clumsy and awkward.

"Very good indeed!" said the teacher when she'd finished.

Angela beamed with pleasure at this praise. "I like it!" she said. "The laws! I love the way it all works by laws."

Eileen O'Malley tapped her head significantly with her finger, and Maura, sitting behind her, gave her hair a good hard yank.

After school, on the way to the bus, Maura asked, "How's your knee?"

Angela looked at her in surprise. Then she looked down at the white dressing.

"It's fine. It's all right. I hardly feel it now."

"You see? It wears off. Once you know that, you can put up with it. Oh, look!" She pulled up before a sweet-shop. "What wouldn't I give for a Crunchie!"

"What are they like?"

"They're like—a hard sponge all made of golden sugar, covered with chocolate."

Angela's mouth began to water.

"Let's have one. I'm hungry."

"I've only the bus money."

"But I'm *hungry*," said Angela rather too loudly.

"Well, that's too bad. You'll have to wait till we get home for dinner."

On the bus, Maura asked, "Did you like school?"

Angela wriggled in her seat.

"Oh yes, I did! I loved it!" she cried. But a few moments later, she had a question. "Why don't all the children like it? Sometimes they made a noise and didn't listen."

"Ah well, some of them haven't much head. And then it's not *all* interesting. I bet even you were bored in some lessons. Everybody is."

"Yes," said Angela thoughtfully. "There was one lesson I didn't like because I couldn't understand it."

"You see? Which was it?"

"The one you called R.K.," said Angela slowly. "What is—R.K.?"

"Religious Knowledge," said Maura. For some reason she felt rather anxious. "P'raps you didn't like it because the sister's a bit old and she mumbles."

"No! It wasn't that. I knew what she was trying to say. But she was telling us all sorts of things that she knew weren't true and other things that she couldn't know whether they were true or not."

"You're not saying the sister's a liar!"

Angela frowned. "Lying's bad," she said. "She wasn't lying. She was . . ." She groped for the right word, as she often did. "Guessing."

"Guessing?" Maura was shocked.

"She was talking about what God *wants*. That's something she can't know anything about. She should only tell you what she *knows*. Or, if it's to do with behaving, she should tell you what *she* wants. She can't speak for God."

"But—but . . ." Maura struggled to explain. "That's what religion *is*. Knowing what God wants."

"Then it's nonsense. That's why I didn't like the lesson. That woman was talking nonsense."

Maura gasped. "But she's a nun!" she exclaimed. "A holy sister!"

Angela burst out laughing—a really loud, joyful sound. Rather like Christmas bells, except there was a bit of naughtiness in it, too.

"Do you want to know who is much nearer to God than she is?" she asked.

"Who is?" asked Maura uneasily. People in the bus were staring.

"Colleen."

Maura stared then, too. She felt dismayed. Saying that poor Coll was holier than Sister Josephine was like—well, like Maura's old idea, that she'd had when she was little, of the most shocking thing you could do, which was going to Mass in your knickers. She turned her face away and stared out of the window and didn't talk to Angela till they got home.

Nine

SHE SOON FORGOT about it in the fun of teaching Angela to cook up a fry, and watching her pleasure in eating it. And after supper, which went just as well as breakfast, with no quarrels or Coll-messes, Ma was in such a mellow mood that she said they could use Kieran's radio.

This was something rare. Along with all Kieran's other things, that radio was not supposed to be touched till he came home (by which time, in Maura's private opinion, it would probably have dropped to pieces). But sometimes Ma would get fed up with the telly and have a fancy to listen to some "proper music."

"It reminds me of your da when he was young, to hear men singing," she said. "Lovely voice he had before the drink roughened it. There's a male-voice choir singing from Dublin. We'll hear it."

Neither Foley nor Maura was exactly sold on male-voice choirs, Irish or not, and each would rather have watched the cartoons. But it would be a treat for Colleen, specially if all the family sat together. She loved that. So Foley ran up and carried the radio carefully down to the living-room. Colleen, when she saw it, banged her hands together and gurgled, "Moo-moo!" which was her word for music. Foley twiddled knobs with a great flourish till he found the right station, and soon the little room was full of the sound of singing.

Colleen sat on the two-seater sofa with Angela beside her. She held her hand and kept patting it, none too gently, but Angela didn't seem to mind. Maura sat by the radio with Darren half-asleep in her arms, breathing in his lovely baby smell. Ma was in the rocker, mending, rocking herself, a little smile on her face which wasn't often there. Only Da and Kieran were missing.

Maura didn't miss Kieran all the time, she didn't even miss Da *all* the time—she was too busy; but at moments like this, it was an ache. She supposed she was too old to sit on his lap now but she could have sat on the floor by his feet and he would have played with her hair . . .

And Ma would be happy! Oh, why did the Provos have to come and talk him into joining them, taking advantage of his feelings at Kieran getting put inside? Thinking he could take Kieran's place in the "army" when his family needed him so much more! Maura had heard her mother saying all this over and over until it was fixed, word for word, in her head.

The choir was singing an Irish ballad that Maura loved. It seemed Colleen loved it too, because she suddenly joined in. She was in tune but off-key and it spoiled it, no doubt of that. Everyone but Angela told her to stop it, but she wouldn't, until Foley, who'd been lying on his back in front of the open fire, lost his temper, jumped up, ran at Colleen on the sofa and hit her.

"Shut your face, you silly oul' *boot!*" he shouted.

Coll let out a bellow. Ma, all in one movement, rocked forward, leaned out of her chair, cuffed Foley's ear and scooped him onto her lap, all before the chair rocked back again.

"Now you sit still and keep quiet or you'll be up til' your bed this minute, so you will!" she said.

Only Maura noticed Angela. She was huddled in the corner of the sofa, all shrunk up like a snail when you poke it, with her head hidden in the cushion. After everything calmed down and the music could be heard again, she slowly uncurled and sat up close to Colleen and stroked her very gently. Colleen stopped crying at once, leaned back and let the music flow over her.

Maura did the same.

She got quite carried away. She was sitting next to the radio, and she kept "creeping" the volume up louder so the wonderful voices would fill her head to bursting, and they seemed to fill her heart too, they were so beautiful . . .

In the midst of the most gorgeous bit, she opened her eyes and then she went stiff. She was almost dizzy by then from the force of the music, so that afterwards it would have been possible for her to think she had dreamed what she saw.

There were two Angelas.

One was sitting on the sofa beside Colleen with a rapt expression on her face as if every part of her was listening. The listening Angela was the one Maura knew; she was wearing Maura's old jeans and jumper and she had a smudge of flour on her eyebrow. Pale and beautiful as she still was, she was by now almost ordinary in Maura's eyes.

But there was another one, not ordinary at all.

Maura couldn't see her very well; she was little more than a bright, trembling light in the air above where the ordinary Angela was sitting. But Maura could see her outlines, white and shining, poised above the sofa, straining upward as if trying to pull away. Just behind her there was a fluttering, vibrating, glistening blur, and there was a sound, too, that Maura could hear distinctly above the swell of the orchestra and choir. The sounds of a bird trapped in a box. The sound of wings, desperately, frantically beating. And on the face of this other Angela was a look of pain and struggle so awful that Maura jumped to her feet.

"Oh, let her free, let her fly!" not knowing to whom she cried.

And at that, everything changed. It was like waking from a bad dream. Her mother slid Foley off her knee and ran to get hold of Maura and ask what had got into her. Angela jumped up too, and the other Angela vanished in a split second as if she had never been there.

Colleen, furious in her turn at having the music interrupted, added to the confusion by letting out a number of dismal, discordant howls.

Maura cried hard for some minutes and then felt very strange, quite weak and queasy, and her mother said she had "taken a turn" and should go off to bed early even though it was Friday night. That meant that for once Maura was going to bed before Foley, which Foley thought was a great joke, until he realized that *he* would have to wash the dishes because Ma had to take Colleen up to bed instead of Maura doing it. Being a boy, Foley was not accustomed to helping in the house.

Maura dropped off to sleep at once, but not for long. When she woke, the house was quiet. She lay listening to the night-sounds, counting them—an occasional car swishing past (it was raining), footsteps hurrying in the street, the next-door's telly and the gurgle of a pipe somewhere in the wall. She did all this with great concentration because she was trying not to think of what she had seen, trying to think it was nothing but a madge. "Madge" was the family word for the kind of made-up story grown-ups sometimes call lies but which is actually your *imag*ination playing games with you.

Some game! She'd never had a madge like that. In fact . . . it wasn't a madge. She'd really seen it. And the disturbing thing was that, apart from her distress, she hadn't been very surprised. It was as if she'd known all the time, right from the beginning almost.

"Angela."

"Yes?"

She had to ask straight out. But it was hard. She didn't think she wanted to be sure.

"Are you—an angel?"

There was a long silence. Then Angela got out of Kieran's bed and came and sat cross-legged on the foot of Maura's.

"You saw," she said. "I knew you must have. No one else did."

"It was so terrible!" Maura felt as if she were going to cry again.

"I'm sorry! You weren't meant to see."

"But you must be so miserable!"

Angela turned her head away.

"I'm not all the time," she said. "It was the music made me feel how—different it is down here."

"But you like it, parts of it, don't you? School, and the Rice Krispies, and—and the bus bumping and things like them'ns?"

"Like it . . . Of course I like it! More than like it. It's wonderful. It's like nothing up there. Up there—" Angela paused, frowned in the darkness, gathered her knees up and put her face down on them for a minute.

Maura watched her pityingly. Fancy being home-sick—for heaven! It'd take more than the taste of fish-fingers to make up for that! Maura'd been stupid to think anything the world had to offer might make an angel happy.

But Angela lifted her head and Maura saw her face shining, not with that special, unearthly glow but just with happiness, though it had pain in it too.

"Maura, you don't understand! I know what you thought just then. But you're wrong! Listen. At first I was all mixed up and didn't know where I was or what had happened, and I couldn't remember anything. I just felt—this—" she touched her body and head—"and it felt like a—a prison. I didn't know how to make it move or talk or what to do with it. But you saw: I learned quickly. And almost at once I began to . . . *enjoy*. Oh, what a lovely word that is! It's so *right*. There's so much joy in being alive! The feelings, the sensations!"

"But isn't it better being an angel?" asked Maura timidly.

"How can you understand what it means to have no body, to be all spirit? Oh, of course it's glorious, I felt it again tonight because the music reminded me—there's music all the time *up there*—but one doesn't *feel* its gloriousness. It just *is*. Here, one feels everything. Feeling is only possible when one has a body."

She wriggled around until she could lean against the wall, straightened her back against it and stretched her legs.

"Oh, that's nice! Just that! Resting my back and stretching my feet! Sleeping! Eating! The air on my face when I'm hot! *Learning* . . . that's the best, like stretching the legs of my mind." Maura giggled, and Angela did too. "And laughing . . . and the feeling when pain goes away . . . No wonder the saints—" She stopped. "But even that isn't the same, if the pain goes away because the body is dead."

She sat quietly for a moment. "I knew about pain and sorrow. Of course I did. In theory. But not through the body. Through the soul. We only know about souls."

"What do souls look like?" asked Maura, bursting with curiosity.

But Angela couldn't explain. "I'm getting more words to use all the time, but I've no words for that. I can only tell you that in math lesson today I remembered how it is. It's like . . . base 2. Yes, or no. Dark, or light. We don't *see* people, their bodies, their—beings. That's why it's all so new and strange to me and I seem so stupid. We only see . . . It's like . . . Well. A new soul is like a star, all bright and perfect. And then, as its owner grows older, it gets dim, and sometimes it turns into a sort of black hole. That's when its owner is—bad, sinful. Or sometimes it brightens up again and—*up there*—the music bursts out—it's not happiness exactly, more rejoicing, a sort of ecstasy. Oh, how can you understand?"

"But you're supposed to be helping!" exclaimed Maura, who was growing a bit impatient. "How can you help if you're just . . . just sitting up there watching souls going on and off like lights?"

"Yes," said Angela slowly. "That's how it suddenly seemed to me. I think that may be why I'm here."

"You mean you asked to come?"

"Asked to come? Asked whom? We're not human. There's no asking. It happened because of a law. Everything does. I—must have—broken a law. Or perhaps I made a new one . . . Oh, I don't know! I just don't know!"

"Try to remember what you did."

"We don't—*do*." But Angela was thinking hard. "I heard the song. Not heard, as you can with ears, but—you know."

"Which song?"

"All things bright and—" Angela began.

"Shhh! You'll wake the house up! At assembly, you mean? So you were there?"

Angela sighed. "Not—*there*. I was sort of—with you, with your spirit. Your spirit was in that song and I got it through that."

"Tuned in, you mean."

"Sort of. And then your spirit, and I, were kind of—opened up by the music, and that old priest was talking and telling you about *us* in his funny, guessing way, how we were there to look after you, and then . . . and then I 'heard' you thinking. About the Troubles, and Kieran, and your da, and your poor ma's problems, and how you'd prayed so often and nothing had got better. You remember yesterday I asked you *why?*"

"Why the bomb and that? So?"

Angela whispered, as if she felt ashamed, "I asked 'why'—up there. I came closer to you than I'd ever been—closer than we are ever supposed to come, I'm sure of that—and when I drew away I was full of your thoughts, I got a hint of what it was like to be mortal, to—have *reasons* to grow dim and black. *Temptation.* And it hurt, like pain, only different, and I sent out a great blazing 'Why?' "

"Good for you! I'd have done the same, so I would!"

"But I shouldn't have done it! It was wrong."

"What's wrong about that?"

"Angels, as you call us, don't ask why. They accept. They don't ask anything, ever. And I did."

Maura, still quite baffled, squeezed Angela's hand comfortingly.

"And you think God was cross with you?"

"No," said Angela, "no. It's not like that. God can't get cross, like a person. That's one of the mistakes Sister Josephine makes, talking as if God gets angry and punishes people . . . I broke a law. But perhaps it was a law that was there to be broken . . . Like the Tree," she said oddly.

"What tree?"

"In the Garden. Never mind about that. Anyway, here I am, and I am loving it and hating it and learning about laws, and what I *cannot* understand is how we angels are supposed to do our jobs, as you'd say, unless we know all *this*." She sat still for a moment in the street-lamp light and then said quietly, "Today I understood about stealing."

"*What?* You'd never—"

"When we were outside the shop and you talked about Crunchies. I was empty. It was awful. And you said I'd have to wait till dinner. And suddenly I knew that if I got hungry enough I'd do almost anything to stop that feeling. You see, to us, sin is just this horrible screeching darkness and souls losing their light and their music. Sin is completely hateful. It can't be understood, by angels, why people do it when they could be good. And there's so little we can do except—*will* our special people to be good, to avoid badness. But of course it isn't enough or there'd *be* no sin and suffering—no dark-star souls."

"Can you do miracles?" asked Maura and then she remembered. "Oh, but of course you can! The wee man who came with my bags. And Coll singing the hymn. And the cornflakes tasting of chocolate . . ." Angela turned her head away sharply. Maura peered round into her face. "What did I say wrong?"

"Those little things are nothing! I'm striving all the time, but all I can manage is these *silly* little things. If only I could really help, really change things! If I could get Kieran out of the Maze, or bring your da home. If I could stop the bombs!" She turned fiercely to Maura. "It wasn't all being homesick that made me try so hard to get free tonight! It was—beginning to *know* what it all means, the *reasons* . . . wanting so desperately to change things . . . Maura? Are you listening?"

Maura was, or at least she was trying to, but her eyelids were drooping despite herself. Angela climbed off the bed and tucked Maura in. She gave her a kiss, too, as Maura had kissed her the night before. The lovely white feeling flowed through

Maura again, though perhaps not quite so strongly as before.

"If you can do little miracles I bet you can do big miracles," she murmured.

"No. I don't think so. Perhaps I'm not meant to. You see—"

"Tell me more in the morning," murmured Maura. And she floated off to sleep.

Ten

Visiting day at the Maze was always a Saturday, and always a bad day for Maura.

Her mother got up very early on that day, to bake Kieran a cake and pack up the rest of his food parcel and then to get herself dressed and tidied for him. The prison being right outside the city, she had a long bus journey. She was usually away four hours or more, and when she came back she was always sad and tired. Maura not only had to look after the house and the others most of the day (though Ma usually took Darren around to a neighbor) but get the lunch.

This time, though, she wasn't dreading it half so much, because of Angela. She woke up that Saturday with a light heart and a feeling of expecting something exciting. She heard movements and sat up in bed. Angela was already awake and dressed and was tidying the room in the most ordinary way possible. She was humming a tune, and it wasn't a hymn-tune, either.

" 'Morning,'' she said, hanging Maura's old dressing-gown on the hook behind the door, and kicking her slippers out of sight under the bed.

"Good morning,'' replied Maura bemusedly. The whole thing seemed much more incredible this morning than last night. An angel sitting on your bed talking about souls and heaven in the middle of the night was one thing; an angel in shabby jeans flinging things cheerfully into drawers and cupboards at seven in the morning was another.

"It's you that's the lazybones this morning,'' said Angela. "I've been up for a long time. Look! Didn't I tidy the room nicely?''

She certainly had. If Maura hadn't watched her actually doing it she might have thought it was another wee miracle. In fact, perhaps it was; Angela had done the tidying-up in a completely human fashion, but the general effect was something more. To Maura's bemused eyes, it seemed as if everything had just been painted; the lino sparkled, the rug looked new, and as for the limp, faded curtains, they were crisp and blowing. All the flowers on them looked as if they'd been freshly picked.

"Get up now, I want to make your bed. These coverlets are so pretty,'' said Angela, picking up Maura's tatty old nylon counterpane which had been her aunty's. She gave it a quick flick (it had been on the floor) and suddenly it was all bright and starchy in the sunlight; even the creases on it were square ones, as if it had just come out of its packet.

Maura jumped out of bed and helped Angela make it. When they had finished they stood back and admired the room.

"It's gorgeous," said Maura, adding shyly, "Thanks."

"Oh, that's nothing," said Angela. She had a new air of confidence this morning. "Now, listen, Maura. What we talked about last night is—"

"A secret. Of course, I knew that."

"Good. It's only because people would think you were making it up. As a matter of fact your mother knows it anyway, deep down. She knew it the minute she saw me."

Maura remembered that moment in the hall.

"Why did she keep saying, 'So like, so like'?"

Angela gazed at her with her serious blue eyes.

"Did she never tell you that you had a twin sister?"

"*What?*"

"You were born a twin. *She* was called Angela. She died when she was just a baby."

"And are you . . ."

Angela smiled. "Well, I think that's what your ma thinks."

Suddenly Maura thought of something.

"Why did nobody at school notice how alike we are?"

"Because they don't see what you see, or what your mother and Colleen see. They all thought I was your cousin. They see I'm like you, but not how much."

"Why *are* you just like me?"

"I suppose because, if I have any body, it can only be a copy of yours. . . . Or perhaps I've got the one your sister should have had. . . . Don't ask me!" she suddenly said very light-heartedly. "I've got one, anyway, and on a lovely day like this, I don't feel like worrying about it."

They went downstairs together and made breakfast. All sorts of little *improvements* kept happening. To begin with, the kitchen, instead of being in a mess from last night when Foley had washed-up, was as sparkling as if Ma had cleaned it. Again, everything looked, if not new, at least lovely and clean. Then the Kellogg's packet from yesterday seemed much fuller of little boxes than it ought really to have been, and the funniest thing was, they were all Cocopops. Various containers, including the bread-bin and the tea-jar, seemed to be fuller than they normally were. The milk-bottle wouldn't pour into the milk-jug at first, Maura had to give it a shake like the ketchup bottle, and when the milk did start to flow it was thick and golden, and tasted as rich as cream on their cereals. But when Ma, who didn't like cream, poured milk for her tea out of the same jug, it came out thin and white the way she liked it.

Everyone commented on the deliciousness of breakfast. Foley ate two packets of cereal; Colleen, crying, "Waa-goo!" with glee, ate three, and still there were a couple left at the end for tomorrow.

Ma, bending at the ancient fridge to put the marge

away (marge which had tasted like best Irish butter) suddenly gave a little cry of surprise.

"Good gracious! Look, there's some sausages at the back here! I must have had them for over a week—and I could have sworn we'd eaten them all! I'll bet they're ready to walk away by now." And she took out a big packet of pork sausages and sniffed them gingerly. "Now would you believe it," she said, "they're all right! I'll cook them for dinner . . . Oh, I wish . . ."

"What, Ma?"

"I was just thinking, how they're Kieran's favorites," she said wistfully. "Ah well. I must be off. Can you two girls take care of things while I'm gone? I've left a shopping list and some money . . . Maura darlin', could you face taking Colleen out for a bit til' the Wee Park? She hasn't had a breath of fresh air since the dear knows when."

Maura's heart sank. Taking Colleen out was, or could be, a terrible trial, especially if there were a lot of people around who didn't know her and would stare and snigger or point at her. Even if they didn't, Maura always felt they were noticing her and pitying or despising her. Oh well.

"I'll take her," she said with a sigh.

"You're a good wee girl," said Ma. On impulse she kissed her. She took Darren next door, then picked up her basket of goodies for Kieran, checked the contents of her old handbag, and was about to leave when there was a knock on the back door.

"Good morning to you, Mrs. Cuddy," said a man

whom Maura had never seen before. "Would you be going visiting?"

"Well! Good morning," said Ma, looking very surprised. "What might you be doing here? I didn't know you lived in this neighborhood."

"I don't, I don't. But I happened to be passing and I thought to myself, maybe Mrs. Cuddy is goin' til the same place I am, and for the same reason, and maybe she'd care for a lift. The car's out the front and it'll save you a bus fare."

Foley's ears pricked up. A car! A car outside their door was a rarity. He ran out of the front door to look.

Ma looked flustered. "That's—that's very kind of you," she said. "Well . . . I'll not say no. But we've hardly exchanged two words on visiting days. How did you know my address?"

"Ah! A little bird told me," said the man, twinkling at her. "I thought it would be nice to have company."

Ma flushed.

"I'll just get my hat," she said, though Maura knew she hadn't meant to wear a hat, just a scarf. The man stood on the doorstep smiling around at them all while she was out of the room.

"What a grand little family Mrs. Cuddy has, certainly," he said genially. "This would be Colleen, and you're Maura—but who might you be?" he said to Angela.

"I'm Angela," said Angela. She was staring at him uneasily.

"A visitor, is it?"

"Yes."

"You're well-named, you're well-named!" he said. Then he looked at Maura, "I hear *you're* quite a little angel too," he said.

"Me?"

"Surely. Your mother sings your praises, says she couldn't manage without you. The way things are, she has a hard row to hoe, so she has. She's a grand woman, your ma, and it's very glad I am she has such a pair of sweet, willing helpers to keep her from working and weeping too much till her man comes home." He gave a deep, sad sigh and cast up his eyes. "When will that be, do you suppose?"

Ma came bustling back, looking much nicer. She'd put a bit of lipstick on, something she didn't usually do until she was actually at the Maze because she liked to smoke on the bus and the lipstick would come off on the cigarettes and go to waste. She never bought any makeup, but Maura had got her some for Christmas from the school Christmas fair and she was making it last. It certainly did wonders for her, Maura thought proudly.

When Ma and the man had gone off in the car, Maura said, "That was nice of you, to fix it so Ma wouldn't have to go by bus."

"I didn't," said Angela.

"You mean, you didn't bring that nice wee man?"

"I never thought of it," Angela said and then added surprisingly, "and if I had, I would have brought someone else."

Angela insisted that they give the house a really

thorough cleaning. Maura had to show her how to use the sweeper, the dustpan and brush, and the feather brush for the ceiling cobwebs. What she liked best was spray-polishing, and doing the windows, making them bright. There was nothing magical about the way the house came clean; they both worked extra hard for it, and if the results were better than usual, Maura put it down to that.

Then it was time to go shopping.

"Can you look after Coll while I do it?" asked Maura.

"Can't we both go, and take her with us?"

"Oh no, we can't take Colleen to the shops! It's too far, and besides . . ."

"Besides what?"

"You can never tell how she'll behave."

Angela turned to Colleen, who was still sitting at the table playing with some crumbs.

"Colleen?"

She looked up vaguely when she heard her name, and then grinned at Angela.

"Would you like to go to the shops?"

She lumbered to her feet at once, nodding eagerly.

"Now you've done it," muttered Maura.

"Will you behave nicely if we take you?"

Colleen almost nodded her head off at this, but Maura said, "She doesn't understand. She only understands odd words. I'm surprised she remembers what a shop is . . . Angela, honest, I don't think we ought—"

But Angela said, "She needs the exercise."

"It'll only make her eat more," grumbled Maura under her breath.

"Eating's one of her pleasures. Come on. I'll look after her."

They walked to the shop, the four of them, Foley trailing behind or rushing ahead. Colleen walked slowly between them, like a fat giant with two little handmaidens holding her arms. She held her face up to the sky and played her game of keeping her eyes closed and just letting herself be led along. When they reached a curb, Maura would stop and say, "Colleen, down," and Colleen, eyes tight closed, would make a huge step, and then chortle all the way across the road until they came to, "Colleen, up," when she would lift her big knee as high as she could and slap her foot on the pavement with an echoing cry of, "Aaaaaaap!"

"Has she always been like this?" asked Angela.

"Oh yes, since she was born."

"How did your parents feel . . . ?"

Maura had never thought about it.

"I expect they thought it was the will of God. That's what Ma says about everything that happens."

"The will of God, is it?" said Angela with an edge to her voice.

"Well, isn't it?" asked Maura, glancing at her sideways across Colleen's great bust. "You should know."

"I don't. It's part of the 'why,'" said Angela. "Now I'm here, the why is like a hammer in my head. But God wouldn't will Colleen to be shut up inside this. I'm sure of that."

They reached the small supermarket and with some difficulty guided Colleen through the doors. Then they fastened her fingers around the handle of a trolley and let her push it along between the shelves, while the girls filled it with the things on Ma's list. Foley kept rushing up to them with his hands full of packets of chocolate biscuits, tins of spaghetti, cartons of banana milk and jars of pickles.

"Oh, come on, Maura, just this once! Just this wee one! *Please* . . ."

But Maura only had so much money and she had to be firm, though Angela looked pleading, and not only on Foley's behalf. She kept picking things up too and saying hopefully, "I wonder what this tastes like," and "Have you ever tried these?" Most of the time Maura would say, "We had some once, they're marvelous," or "You'll have to wait for Christmas or a birthday for a bite of that."

"But that lady's got some in her basket, why can't we . . . ?"

Maura sighed. She had nagged her mother so often for extras, and now the others were nagging *her*, and she had to be firm and responsible, or she'd run out of money.

"What other people buy is no concern of ours," she said in a no-nonsense voice. "Come on, Coll, keep moving."

Colleen had come to a stop opposite the biscuit shelves. She was eyeing the lovely packets hungrily.

"Bik?" she said longingly. "Collabik?"

"No. You can't. Come on, shake yourself." Maura

tried to urge Colleen into moving, but she stood there like the Rock of Gibraltar.

"Bik," she said again, but with no question-mark this time. Her bland blue eyes had gone narrow, the way Maura's did when she was determined.

Maura read the danger-signals and her heart sank. She turned to Angela, who was wistfully examining a packet of Wagon Wheels.

"It was your idea to bring her, now please get her away from the biscuits," she said, trying to keep a shrill note of desperation out of her voice.

Angela turned to Colleen with her sweetest smile.

"Come along, darlin'," she said. (She seemed to be losing her angel accent.)

Colleen looked at her but she didn't move. "BIK," she said, so loudly this time that several heads turned. And she reached out for a packet on the shelf.

Maura quickly put a packet of Rich Tea biscuits into her hand. "It's the only way," she said before Angela could protest. "Come on now, Coll!"

But Coll had no intention of coming anywhere. She held the packet deliberately over the trolley, opened her fingers wide to let it drop in, gave them all a look of triumph, and reached for a packet of chocolate digestives.

Foley giggled, and Maura, who felt suddenly quite frantic inside, took a swipe at him. Angela didn't notice. She seemed to be concentrating on Colleen with all her might. Colleen was ignoring her. Packet after packet was seized, held over the trolley, and dropped in. Maura knew better than to try to stop her physically, but Angela didn't—she laid a restraining hand on her arm. Colleen stopped dead for a moment, then shook her off violently and went right on, grabbing biscuits, this time using both hands.

"Oh, what'll we do?" moaned Angela, her confidence collapsing. "Why won't she stop?"

"Why don't you stop her—you know how—" said Maura frantically.

"I've tried! I can't reach her!"

Suddenly the thing Maura had been trying to prevent happened. She lost her temper. She knew it was a fatal thing to do with Colleen, but the sight of the overflowing trolley snapped something inside her.

"Coll! Stop that! Stop, do you hear, or I'll slap you, so I will!"

At the sound of Maura's anger, Colleen opened her mouth and yelled, "NAAAAAAAA! Ba-mor!" And she swung the flat of her big hand round, hitting a tall pyramid of tins of soup, which crashed to the ground. Everyone in the shop seemed to come running. All except one—Angela. She *went*.

She just fled, around the corner of the displays and out of sight. Foley swiftly followed her example. Maura stood there, her blood beating in her head with rage and shame, wanting to box Colleen's ears first and fall through the floor right afterwards.

Colleen, however, just stood stock-still looking at the tumbling, rolling tins. There were a few left in their places; she knocked those off too, but without conviction. Then she looked around at the crowd of people and the angry faces of the assistants. She turned to Maura and sort of folded over on top of her until her face was hidden on Maura's shoulder.

Eleven

"BA'COLL," SHE WHISPERED tearfully. "Sollycoll."

Maura shook her off. "It's no use being sorry," she said. "I've got to pick them all up now, haven't I?" She bent, hiding her red face, and began helping the assistants who were grumblingly setting up the pyramid again. Her hands were trembling. When she stood up and looked around, she was astonished to see Coll trying to cram all her packets of stolen biscuits back on their shelf. Her tears were freely flowing.

The crowd had gone about its business. They were alone again. Maura got out a grubby hanky and wiped her sister's face with it and made her blow her nose, which she was quite good at. "All right, Coll," she said gently. "Better now." She helped her fit the packets back neatly, and then, at the last minute, took one back.

Colleen's woebegone face brightened. "Swee'coll?"

"That's right. Not that you deserve it."

She got Colleen moving again without problems, and they finished their shopping. She had begun to seethe with anger again inside, and not because of Colleen this time. The cause, Angela, was waiting by the check-out, with Foley beside her. She was gazing at the floor and did not look up as Maura reached her.

"So there you are!" said Maura in a furious undertone. "A fine guardian angel you turned out, so you did! Just when I need you, you're running off around corners as fast as your legs'll carry you! If you'd had your wings, no doubt you'd have been away faster!"

Angela hung her head lower than ever. Her shoulders gave a heave.

"Now don't you start!" said Maura, sounding, even to herself, more like her ma every moment. "It's no use girnin' over spilled milk. Go over there til' that pile of boxes and fetch me a couple of nice little ones and help me pack up the shopping. Paul, go and help her." She only called Foley "Paul" when she was boiling mad. They went, like a pair of smacked puppies. Maura began rapidly lifting the things out of the basket and was surprised to find Colleen almost helping, at least as much as she could, while holding her biscuits tightly to her chest.

They walked most of the way home in silence. Even Foley trotted at their heels and didn't let a peep out of him.

"It was the noise," said Angela after a long time, in a wee, tiny voice.

"Oh, sure! You hate noises, don't you? Well, I told you. You'll have to learn to put up with them."

Angela said nothing more until they were nearly home. Then suddenly she stopped. She just stood there in the middle of the street, her face almost in the box of groceries she was carrying.

Maura stopped too. "What's up wit' you now?" she asked, still cross. Angela said something so softly she couldn't hear it. *"What?"*

"I feel so bad."

"What do you mean? Are you ill?"

Angela shook her head and gave a deep sniff.

"Are you hungry?"

Again, a shake and a sniff. "It's another kind of pain. I keep thinking about—running away—and I feel—just—terrible! It's worse than when I hurt my knee."

Something like a laugh twitched at Maura's mouth.

"Oh, so that's it! That's nothing but your conscience eatin' you. And so it should as well."

Angela raised her tear-stained face, white and agonized.

"I want to go home!" she gasped.

Maura chose to misunderstand her.

"We're nearly there. Here, Foley, you carry her box for a bit."

But Angela wouldn't give it to him. She just pushed on up the street, head down. Maura gave Foley her box and paused to haul poor Coll, who hadn't walked so far for ages, up the last fifty yards. She called after Angela, "Will you stop girnin' into the greens! Have you no hanky?"

When they all got back into the house Maura had to show Angela how to blow her nose, which needed it more than Colleen's. Then she gave Colleen and Foley their cold lunch. She was starving hungry herself, which meant that Angela probably was too, but Angela wouldn't eat.

Maura knew exactly what she was feeling. She herself often refused to eat when her mother was angry with her or when she felt guilty. She tried to do as her mother did—ignore the whole thing, knowing no one ever starves to death from missing one meal. But after a bit she found she couldn't eat either, if Angela didn't. She could feel Angela's misery in her own chest, and her throat closed up.

"Will you stop it now?" she said, laying down her cold fish-finger that she'd been eating in her fingers, dipped in ketchup. "You're spoiling my lunch, so you are. Look, you're even making Coll sad." Indeed, Colleen was gazing at Angela open-mouthed, eyes bulging with tears. Only Foley was gobbling away, unmoved.

At this Angela pushed back her chair and rushed upstairs. Maura, following with a sigh, found her face down on her bed.

Maura sat on the edge and patted her uneasily. Knowing that she was really an angel seemed to make the situation more complicated. Obviously she would feel worse than any ordinary person about doing wrong or running away or just not doing her job—"failing in her duty," Da would say.

"I understand how you feel," said Maura, "but it's

not as bad as you think. It happens all the time. My da told me that once in the war, *his* da ran from the fighting, and they caught him, and he was court-martialed. D'you know what that means?"

A shake of the head.

"Well, it's the worst thing that can happen to a soldier, so it is. They were goin' to shoot him only the war ended. He never got over it. But my da said we're all cowards at heart. When you're facing what you can't face, there's always a chance you might turn and run." It was strange to hear herself talking like this, so grown-up—Maura hadn't known she had it in her. But she'd changed since Angela came. She knew more inside herself, about living, not just about school things. And she could say them better, too.

Angela was sitting up and wiping her poor swollen eyes. "I—I thought I was hurt when I banged my knee," she gasped, "but sure I'd rather be killed to *death* than feel again what I feel now." She blew her nose. "How could I have run and left you? Left Colleen? I don't know what happened to me, so I don't!"

"Well, I know well enough! I wanted to run away myself. That's why I didn't want Colleen to come. You never know how she might shame you or cause trouble. Not that she means to."

"I was so sure," said Angela, putting her feet on the floor.

"Sure of what?"

"Myself, I suppose. Sure I could control her—reach her. I did it before, remember?—at the table. And in the living-room. I only had to touch her and she was like a lamb. But in the shop, I was *willing* her to be good, and nothing happened! Nothing. You know— I think if I'd stayed, and not run away, I could have made all those tins jump back into their places, if I'd tried hard enough. But I couldn't get to Colleen."

"Oh, sure. She's stubborn as an oul' donkey when she gets in a mood. And if you get cross with her she's worse. I shouldn't have said I'd slap her. She goes a bit wild when you don't love her."

Angela was looking at her oddly.

"Of course," she said. "Anybody would."

They sat in silence for a moment. Then Angela stood up.

"Let's go down and eat," she suggested.

Too late! All the fish-fingers had vanished down the throats of Foley and Colleen. Both girls were disappointed, but they looked at each other, and at the ketchup-covered faces of the two at the table, and couldn't help laughing.

"Let's have bread and jam instead."

They were just tucking in when they heard running footsteps up the back path. Maura's head jerked up.

"That's Ma! Why's she running?"

She jumped up just as Ma threw the door open. She looked wild. Her hat was askew and her hair all over the place and she was flushed and shiny from hurrying.

"Ma! What's wrong?"

"It's your brother," she gasped. "He's out!"

Twelve

ANGELA REGISTERED THE news before Maura. She jumped up from her place with a cry of delight and began clapping her hands. Colleen seemed to think it was a party, and joined in with loud "Maaaa's" and "Aaaa's."

But Maura was looking at her mother's face and saw nothing there to rejoice at.

"How d'you mean, out?" And then suddenly, her hands flew to her mouth. "Holy God, Ma! He's never escaped!"

Her mother nodded her head and sank into a chair. A silence fell. Maura automatically moved to the stove to put on the kettle, but her mother stopped her with a single gesture—she pointed at the cupboard beneath the sink, and Maura changed direction. Her heart was in her boots. If Ma wanted a drink of whisky instead of tea, then things could hardly be worse.

She poured the strong-smelling stuff out carefully and handed it to her mother, who took a big swallow and then leaned back with her eyes closed. Angela, without a word, hiked Colleen out of her chair and led her from the room. It needed an angel, Maura thought, to be so tactful; it wouldn't be so easy to get rid of Foley, who was already bursting with questions.

"Where's Kieran, Ma, did he get out, is he coming home, are they after him?"

"Keep quiet, Foley! Why don't you go out and play?" hissed Maura.

"Don't want to! Where's Kieran, Ma?"

She opened her eyes and looked from one to the other. "How do I know?" she said wearily, and drank another mouthful of whisky. "He's got out, that's all they'd tell me. Has there been anybody here?"

"We were out all the morning, shopping," said Maura. She felt much more stunned than she had when the bomb went off. This was a family explosion and hit her much harder than any ordinary one. And something else was bothering her; she couldn't think just what it was. Something to do with Angela.

"Was it only him that broke out?" she asked.

"I don't know. Them'ns wouldn't tell me a thing. They said he'd got out early this morning and I was to go home straight and wait. Oh," she moaned, "what'll I do, what'll I do? Sure and he wouldn't be such an eejit as to come home, that's the first place they'll be watchin'!" She suddenly turned to look over her shoulder at the window, and ricked her neck. "Ow! Maura. Go through to the living-room and peep through the nets to see if you can spot anyone watching the house. Look right to the ends of the street, mind."

Maura did as she was told. All the windows had thick, nylon-net curtains hanging in them. Moving them as little as possible, she peeped out, first one way and then the other. She couldn't see anyone who looked as if he was just hanging about.

"There's no one there, Ma," she called.

"There will be."

As Maura came back into the kitchen her mother levered herself up from her chair. All the makeup was gone and she looked ill and old. Maura ran to her and gave her a hug.

"It's all right, darlin'," Ma said, patting her. But it was far from all right and Maura knew it. They looked at each other and they were both thinking the same thing: *If only Da were here!*

They spent the next few hours in a state of awful suspense. They talked in jerks when they thought of something to say. There was no flow, no ease of conversation. Foley whined and asked questions and got on everyone's nerves. Angela stood aside. She did things to help as they were needed, but at other times she just stood against a wall with her eyes on the floor and her hands behind her back. All you could see was her hair falling over her bent face.

"Did that fella bring you home?" Maura thought to ask at dinner time when nothing new had happened.

"Which fella?"

"The one who came to pick you up this morning. Who was he, anyhow?"

"Oh, him! That's Mr. O'Dowd. I see him sometimes on visitin' days. He must have a boy of his own inside . . . Funny him comin' like that . . . I could swear I'd never give him my address or said more than a good-day to him."

"He's a bit young to be having a big son," said Maura.

Her mother threw her a funny look. "So he is," she said. "I never thought of it . . . Ah well, some of them's get married straight from school." But she seemed troubled. "He asked a lot of questions . . . about your da and when I last seen him. Oh, Maura love, you don't think he's a tout?"

"Of course not!" Maura said at once, just because it was what Ma wanted to hear. Then she spoiled it by adding, "Anyhow, you wouldn't tell him anything."

"I don't know—I don't know—not on the way I didn't, I was myself then. But he did drive me home after I'd been given the news of Kieran and then I was out of my wits entirely. I might have said anything . . ."

"Ma, you didn't! Not about Da bein' with the Provos!"

Her mother began to pace the floor, wringing her hands. "He seemed so kind, helping me into his car, and giving me all the soft talk about how brave I was, the way I was takin' the news, and how badly I'd feel the lack of a man to share my burden . . . Oh Jesus, Mary and Joseph, what did I say to him?"

Maura glanced at Angela. Her head was up now and she was listening, an anxious frown between her eyes.

"What's up wit' you?" Maura whispered to her.

Angela shook her head, but the frown didn't vanish; it deepened.

Soon afterwards the neighbor who had been looking after Darren came to bring him back. Her name was Mrs. Dooley and she was kind, but what Da used to call "terrible heavy on the dramatics." She loved gossip and she made a big tarara out of everything. Now her face was all lit up with excitement.

"It was on the news!" she whispered, as if someone might be listening. "Think of that, your boy tying up the priest and walkin' out in his clo's! Who'd have thought he'd lay hands on a man of the cloth! Of course, it's like I always said, that's the trouble with puttin' them's in jail, they get intil' terrible bad company! And now he's a fugitive and the dear knows when or if you'll ever see him again alive—"

Maura, looking sideways, saw Angela make a face, a most unangel-like face with all her white teeth showing, and Mrs. Dooley suddenly clutched her leg.

"Oh, Holy Mother, what a twinge! It's my bunions, they're givin' me stabs even when I'm takin' the weight off me feet. They never let up on me! Ow, ooooh, this is the worst they've been for a week! I'd best be goin' home and put on my slippers, these shoes are killin' me." And she tottered out through the back door.

But her words had hit home. Ma was sitting with her head in her hands at the kitchen table.

"Dear God, what possessed him? Why couldn't he stay put? But then he was always willful and headstrong. They shouldn't have tried shuttin' him up, I knew he'd never stand it—"

"He stood it fine for two years," interrupted Maura, very upset. "Go up and lie down a bit. Take a pill or something, please!"

"I can't rest! What if—?"

But then Angela came and put her hand on Ma's arm and said, "Try, please. Just try!" And it worked this time. Ma smiled at her through her tears and without another word got up and went out of the room. They heard her weary footsteps going slowly up the stairs.

Foley trailed off to watch TV. Maura took Darren out of his pram and sat with him asleep in her arms. Angela was standing over by the sink, looking out into the twilight as if she were waiting for something. After a while she said, "You might as well start cooking the sausages."

It seemed an odd remark in the circumstances.

"But we've had dinner."

"You'd better cook them just the same."

Maura started to object, but then she thought that a hot sausage might be just the thing to make them all feel a bit better. So she laid Darren back in his pram and fished the packet out of the fridge and put the frying-pan on the gas. She pricked the skins of the fat sausages and before long there was a lovely, savory sizzle in the air.

Knowing how much Angela enjoyed trying new things to eat, and since it had been her idea, Maura kept glancing at her, expecting her to turn from the window in answer to that mouth-watering smell. But she just stood absolutely still, staring out. It was nearly dark . . . Suddenly she said, without turning, "Maura! Take a sausage up to Colleen."

There was such urgency in her voice that Maura obeyed without thinking. She speared a hot sausage onto a bit of soda-bread, rolled it up, and carried it, oozing fat, up the stairs.

Peeping into Ma's room she saw her under her eiderdown, fast asleep. Good! Then she went into her own room, or what had been hers until Angela came, the room she had shared all her life with Colleen.

The room was almost dark. Maura stopped in surprise. Colleen, instead of sitting as she usually did, hour after hour, in her chair by the window, was standing up. Her big form was blocking the street light through the window and it looked as if she were actually watching something.

Colleen's long periods up here by the window used to puzzle Maura when she was younger. Then she decided that Colleen's brain, what there was of it, was like a radio. If nobody was there to switch it on, it was just unplugged-in, silent—demanding nothing and giving out nothing. Coll would only begin to fuss if she got cold or hungry—loneliness and boredom didn't seem to worry her. Nor did she ever seem to react to things going on in the street.

That's why Maura was so astonished to see her standing looking out.

When Maura came up behind her with the sausage, Colleen, without turning, pointed down and said, quite clearly, "Man."

Maura became cold all over. Pushing past Coll's bulk she twitched the net curtain and looked out. First she looked left, up the hill to the end of the short, narrow street.

Sure enough, there he was—on the far side, leaning on the end-wall with the picture of the hunger-striker and the Virgin Mary.

Maura's heart almost stopped. She looked the other way. Yes! There was another one at the other end. "Holy Mother of God . . ." she whispered. Then, still clutching the sausage, she ran to the head of the stairs and called softly,

"Angela!"

"What is it?" came Angela's silvery voice from the kitchen.

"There's men watching the ends of the street!"

A moment later she heard the back door close.

She ran down the stairs and into the kitchen. Angela was gone. Opening the back door, Maura was just in time to see her disappear through the gate in the high brick wall that separated their yard from the alley. Maura opened her mouth to call after her, but her voice just wouldn't come out.

She stood there, frozen with an awful feeling of fear.

Darren woke up in his pram and began to cry.

Maura put down the sausage, picked him up and cuddled him. It did her good to hold him, all sweet with sleep. It calmed her down. But after a while he stopped crying, grew red in the face, and after that he didn't smell so sweet any more. So she changed him on the floor and then dragged his play-pen into the living-room where Foley was sitting on the floor in front of the TV. The fire was out and the room was cold.

"Oh, don't bring him in here, I don't want him!" Foley moaned.

"It won't hurt you to mind him for a bit. He's your little brother as much as mine," said Maura sharply.

"But I'm watching *Magpie!*"

"It's two for sorrow, then," retorted Maura smartly.

Foley looked baffled.

"Well, can I have a sausage?"

"I suppose so."

"In a bun?"

"We've no buns. Wrap it in a bit of soda-bread."

While Foley made a rather messy copy of a hot-dog, Maura took Colleen's back up to her. She was sitting down again now, as if she'd done what she had to. She beamed when she saw the sausage. "Coll goo!" she said.

"Yes, you're a very good girl," said Maura. "You told Maura about the man." She didn't expect a response to this, but Coll surprised her again. Her mouth full of sausage, she said, "Ba maaa."

"Bad? How do you know—?" But that was useless. She patted her sister uneasily and went out.

And now Maura was, to all intents and purposes, alone.

If Angela had not been Angela, she would have been very worried about her, out there alone in the night. As it was, she could think of nothing but Kieran. What must it be like to run away from prison, to have your name on the radio and television, to have everyone on the hunt for you, trying to catch you and drag you back?

Thirteen

MAURA SWITCHED OFF the television and dragged Foley to bed by main force. Only the promise of a story stopped him from bringing the roof down at being put to bed so early.

The story of course had to be about an angel who came to life and could do wonderful things. She could do anything you asked her to. When it was Foley's birthday, she gave him a magic ice-lolly that lasted all day, and at night she took the lollystick and planted it in a pot, and in the morning it had grown into a tree in the back yard, right to the top of the brick wall. It had all sorts of wonderful things growing on it—anything Foley wanted. He only had to climb up into the lolly-tree and ask, and it would pop out of one of the branches.

"Could it make a Crunchie?"

"It made Crunchies before you'd even asked," said

Maura. "It could do much better than that! It wasn't just things to eat. It made him new jeans and roller-skates and a big picture-book and a baby hamster and—"

"Bik?" came a little voice from the other bed. "Swee?"

Maura swung around in astonishment. Colleen was lying on her side, her eyes fixed on Maura, and if she wasn't listening, she certainly looked as if she was trying to.

"Yes! Biscuits and sweets, and flowers, and—"

"Moo?"

"Yes! A radio, playing lovely music for you, Coll!"

"I want it to make a bicycle," said Foley.

"Yes, and a—" But then Maura stopped. Her madge boggled at the thought of a *bicycle* hanging from a tree. "No," she said flatly, "it couldn't make a bike."

"Why not?" he asked querulously. "You said *any*thing."

"Well—Foley wanted a bike, and he sat in the tree and asked it to make him one. But nothing happened. So he got very, very cross, and started kicking the tree and shaking its branches,"

"Bam! Bam! Baaa!" cried Colleen excitedly.

"Yes," said Maura slowly, watching her in wonder. Surely she wasn't *understanding* the story? "He *was* bad, and the tree suddenly started to jump about. It threw him right off with a wallop on his—"

"Bum!" shouted Coll. That was an accident, of course; she still meant "bam." But Foley burst out laughing.

"And when he got up, guess what?" Maura's unruly audience fell into an awed silence. Maura was amazed at herself. How the ideas kept coming! "The tree had shriveled right up, so it had, and there was the old lollystick stuck in the pot, as normal as normal."

"Did all the things shrivel up, too?" asked Foley, looking rather shamefaced about having kicked the tree.

Maura opened her mouth with a stern expression, but then she looked into Foley's beseeching eyes. Things never seemed to turn out in life as you wanted them to. Why should stories always be strictly according to the rules? "No. The ground was covered with Crunchies and toys and things. And the music was still playing. But Foley knew he'd been greedy. So he picked up the Crunchies in Ma's shopping basket and asked the angel to give them to poor children."

"*All* of them?"

"Yes," said Maura sternly. But then she relented. "She gave two back, one for Foley and one for Coll."

"Sweecoll," remarked Colleen dreamily.

She rolled over on her back and put her thumb in her mouth. She was always doing it, and it never failed to irritate Maura.

"Take your thumb out, Coll!" she said, for about the millionth time, without the slightest hope.

Colleen turned her head, looked at Maura and took her thumb out of her mouth.

"Collgoo," she said. "Kithcoll."

Maura leaned over her bed and kissed her.

"Goodnight, Colleen," she said, as she had said so many times before without getting the slightest response. But tonight was so strange that she was hardly even surprised when Colleen replied obligingly, "Ni Mor."

"She's talking," said Foley from his bed.

"Not really," said Maura, but she wasn't so sure.

When she bent over to kiss Foley, he whispered, "Will Kieran come?"

Maura shivered. "I hope not," she said. "They'll catch him sure, if he does."

No sooner had she come down the stairs when she had a strong impulse to re-heat the sausages, now settling into their grease. And no sooner had she done that than she heard a scratching on the back door. It was Angela, crouching low, and when Maura opened the door she scuttled in like a crab.

"Turn off the lights!" she whispered urgently.

"Why? Where've you been?"

"I had to warn him . . . he's in the yard now."

Maura gasped.

"How—how did you—?" But then she remembered. There were things Angela still knew, could still do, even if she couldn't do big miracles. "You shouldn't have brought him here!" she exclaimed.

"Do you think I wanted to? I couldn't stop him! We crept around the back over some walls. He's not eaten all day . . . Are the sausages ready?"

"Yes," said Maura, beginning to get excited.

Kieran! She hadn't seen him since his trial, except twice when Ma had taken her to visit. Her big brother, the hero! Her da had said, when the Brits had come to take him and Maura had cried and cried, "Never you mind, darlin'. It's a hero you've got for a brother! He's paid them back for that rifle-butt in the teeth, so he has!"

And here the hero came, creeping around the door like a thief.

Before Maura could get a good look at him, he had sprung like a big cat at the switch by the door, and the next moment the room was dark. But she had caught a glimpse. He was thin and sweating and dirty. His face was exhausted; he looked scared to death. And he was dressed like a priest.

"Maura," he whispered into the darkness. "I'm done. Give me some food and a drop of whisky." And he slumped into a chair at the table.

Groping in the dark, she managed to carry the whole frying-pan to the table and put it in front of him. He crouched over it, a bent silhouette against the faint light from the window. Maura saw Angela get out the whisky bottle and pour some into a cup from the sink. She heard Kieran curse as he burned his fingers, and it crossed her mind that all this must seem very far from heaven to Angela.

Kieran began to eat and drink ravenously, like an animal. Angela's hand crept into Maura's. It was icy cold and Maura could feel her shivering.

"Maybe I should wake Ma," whispered Maura. "I wish Da was here!"

"Don't," muttered Angela. "Oh, don't!"

"Don't what?"

"Wish. Don't wish so hard."

After a moment she added in a thin, high voice, "I did it."

"Did what? What are you talking about?"

But Angela wouldn't answer. She just stood there in the dark looking at Kieran.

When he'd taken the edge off his appetite and drunk the whisky he leaned back in the chair. He put his head back and made a sound like a groan.

Maura crouched by him and held his arm.

"How'd you get out, Kieran? How'd you ever get out?"

For a moment or two he was perfectly still. Then he leaned forward and stuffed the last sausage, whole, into his mouth.

"I saw my chance and I took it," he mumbled shortly. He chewed and swallowed. Then he turned to face Maura. "I must've been mad. I had it easy in there. I was earning remission off my sentence with good behavior. I had privileges . . . And then suddenly, this morning, when the father came early to take confessions, somethin' came over me. Like a— an irresistible urge to get til' home, as if something was dragging at my arm. And before I knew what I was doin' I'd grabbed a blanket and thrown it over the man's head. God forgive me! I tied him up with the arms of my shirt, so I did, after threatenin' to harm him if he didn't strip off his cassock . . ."

Kieran looked down wonderingly at the priest's

black robe he was wearing, and touched the once-white, now soiled and crumpled dog-collar. "I tell you I didn't know what I was doing!" he burst out. "I've done some things, but I'd never harm a man of God! Not in my right senses! The devil was at work in me to make me do such a mad thing—"

Angela gasped and hid her face, but Maura scarcely noticed.

"So you dressed in his clothes. Then what?"

"What triggered me off to do it was, one of the others in my 'cage' had nudged me when he come in—the father, I mean—and said he looked like me, and so he did. With the big hat on, none of the guards knew the difference, and I just walked through. It was like a miracle."

At this, Maura did look at Angela. A sudden, terrible thought had come to her. Angela stood there with her face in her hands, perfectly still.

"Angela—?" she began. But Kieran was still talking.

"And the miracle went on. The man on the big gate, when he saw me coming, stopped me, and I thought, this is it—I was almost glad—but what he said was, 'You left your keys in your car, Father. You're too trusting! Here, I've got them safe for you.' And he handed them to me and waved his hand at a wee oul' Mini parked nearby, and I just—got in and drove away."

"Why did you come back here? Don't you know it's the first place they'll look?"

"I know it!" moaned Kieran despairingly. "I tell you, something seemed to be pullin' me til' home."

Maura was still looking at Angela.

"Maybe they won't catch you," she said slowly.

"Don't be stupid! Of course they will. How can they help it? This one here—" he indicated Angela with his thumb—"come out to meet me and we dodged and hid and climbed walls—I've seen nothin' like the way she climbs, for a wee girl she's a wonder, she was up and over as if she'd a pair of wings, and me after her . . . Maybe if she hadn't come, I'd have been caught by now and it'd all be over, so it would . . ."

But Maura had stopped listening at the word "wings." She had suddenly understood.

This was Angela's doing. All day, since Ma returned, she had been acting strangely, as if she were on tin-tacks—waiting. She *knew* what was going to happen *because she'd made it happen.*

Kieran abruptly stopped speaking.

"Oh God," he said hollowly, "I'm goin' to be sick . . ."

He lurched to his feet, tipping his chair over backwards, and ran out of the room and up the stairs.

Maura turned on Angela in the dark kitchen.

"Why did you do it!" she cried accusingly.

Angela's still figure began to shake with sobs.

"You wanted it," she mumbled through her fingers. "I tried to *help!*"

"I didn't want it this way! Don't they ever teach you anything up there? Don't you know things don't ever happen nicely, the way you want them to? You must be simple in the head after all! I suppose you just said a prayer, 'Let Kieran come home from jail!' "

Angela uncovered her face and Maura could see her great, wet eyes staring at her.

"But that's what you say, in your prayers!"

That stopped Maura short, because it was true. She had been guilty of saying prayers like that, unthinking, stupid prayers that couldn't possibly come true. Fairy wishes, like bikes on lolly-trees. Childish. Impossible.

Could God change the rules just for her? Of course not! Angela certainly should have known that, but Maura should have known it, too. Angela knew more about "up there," perhaps, but Maura knew more about what happened down here.

Maura went and put her arm around Angela.

"All right. Stop crying. It's happened. Now we've got to think what to do."

Fourteen

WHEN KIERAN CAME back down from the bathroom, the girls were waiting for him in the hall.

"Come into the living-room," whispered Maura. "We've pulled the curtains. We can have the light on and you can rest a bit while we think what's best to do."

They led him in, sat him on the sofa and put his feet up on the tuffet Foley sat on to watch TV. He really did look done-in, but at least he'd had a wash and changed into his ordinary clothes. He'd even run a comb through his black curly hair, Maura noticed. That was like the old Kieran. Forever combing his hair and admiring himself in the mirror . . . But now his good looks were spoiled by thinness, the sick, yellow color in his skin, the shadow of a beard on his narrow jaw—and most of all, by his scared, hunted expression.

"Where's Ma?" he asked suddenly.

"She's upstairs asleep."

"Good. Good. Don't wake her. I'll be off soon enough, it's best if she don't see me." He leaned back and closed his eyes. He didn't look as if he'd be off anywhere.

"Where will you go?"

"When you're on the run, God alone knows where you'd best be heading."

"Can't you stay here?"

"It's a wonder they're not beatin' me into the ground already. I don't know how I got here without them spottin' me." His eyes closed and his head fell back against the sofa. In a few moments his mouth dropped ajar and he began to snore so loudly that Maura thought the watchers outside the house must hear him.

Angela was sitting in Ma's rocker staring at him. She had stopped crying earlier, but now Maura was disturbed to see new tears streaming silently down her pale cheeks.

"What is it?" Maura whispered. "What you crying for?"

"Why is the world so hard?"

"Da says there's nothing wrong with the world, it's just the bad people in it." Then she wished she hadn't said "bad people." Angela might think she meant Kieran. She wished he hadn't come back, not just for his sake, but for hers . . . She'd rather Kieran was a hero, in prison, than a poor, hunted man out of it, looking no sort of hero at all.

And what must Angela feel? She was blaming herself, though she'd meant everything for the best. She sat there, staring at Kieran's sprawling, sleeping figure, as if willing him to vanish, to be back again in the Maze, for it to be this morning before it all happened. . . .

In the suspenseful silence, Maura's mind wandered, seeking escape from the awful situation. She found herself thinking of a film she'd seen recently. Superman had made the world spin backward to save his girlfriend's life. . . . That part had bothered Maura. Superman's father had told him not to change history, and he had broken the rule. And Maura had waited for him to lose his powers, to be punished somehow, but the film-makers had allowed him to get away with it. Even in a film, Maura had felt, there ought to be penalties for breaking a rule like that.

"You can't undo it, can you?" she whispered.

"No."

"What can you do, then?"

"I'm keeping those men from coming to the door," Angela said in a faraway voice. "That's all I can think of at the moment. But Maura—something else may be going to happen."

Holy God! Something more?

"When we were talking last night, about the things I wanted to change, I . . . I mentioned something else."

"Da," Maura breathed. "You don't think . . . ?"

"Maybe."

"But that'd be—great! If Da was here, he'd know what to do!"

"Would he?"

"But—but if Da marches down the street, they'll catch the both of them, so they will!"

"That's what I'm frightened of."

"Angela, couldn't you make those men outside go away?"

"They've got their rules too," Angela said strangely.

"I know. But maybe you could—"

"I'm afraid!" Angela burst out suddenly, so that Maura shushed her.

"Afraid of what?"

"Striving for things. Things that weren't meant to happen. Look at Kieran. If I did that, it was terrible. A terrible mistake. I've learned my lesson. Even if I had a lot more power than I have . . . Even if I were . . ."

"An archangel, you mean? Or—"

"An archangel would have been wiser."

"How d'you know? Maybe they don't know any more about the world and why the bad things happen than *you* do. Than you *did*," she amended.

Angela shook her head.

"Sometimes now I've got a body, I long for something without remembering it might change things . . . Break the rules. Like my 'why.' " She looked at Maura with anxious eyes—how different now from that blank, baby-like look she had had at first. It occurred to Maura that she might be more person now than angel. "You see, I'm so afraid," she went on in a low voice. *"Now.* I'm scared. I know something really awful will happen if those men come in here looking for Kieran. I can't *help* wishing your da were here to look after us. And my wishing—I can't hold it back—it's the same as striving to change things.''

At that moment, something happened that made both the girls leap out of their chairs. Kieran came awake with a jarring start which, as he jumped to his feet straight from sleep, made him stumble dizzily.

"What was that!" cried Angela, putting her fingers to her ears as if in pain.

"Shootin'. That's what that is," said Kieran grimly. "And it's close. Douse the light." Maura put the light off and Kieran knelt on the sofa and twitched the curtains. Then, in a flash, he had clapped them together again with his two hands. At the same time they heard heavy, booted feet running past the house.

"Number one's gone, and there goes number two from up the road," Kieran breathed. "Gone to see what's goin' on . . . Maybe it's some real action, and maybe it's a diversion."

"What's that?" whispered Maura in terror. She found she was huddling in the corner right behind the television.

"A noise to make them run away from where the real action is," said Kieran. "I wonder, could some of my pals on the outside have come to slip me away? No, that's impossible! How could they dream I'd come *here*?" Another series of single shots made the three of them freeze. Maura found herself racing through Hail Marys while her heart hammered in her chest.

Suddenly she thought of her mother. She stopped praying and, wriggling out from behind the TV, ran out of the room and up the stairs. She found Ma sitting bolt upright in her bed, stiff as a board, staring as if she didn't know where in the world she was or what was going on.

"Maura? Maura? Is that you?" she called sharply.

"Yes, Ma. It's me. Don't be gettin' excited."

Now there's a silly thing to say, she thought. She sat on the edge of the bed and held her mother's hands. "Listen, though. Kieran's home!"

"What? And me up here, sleepin' like a pig?" She almost shoved Maura aside and jumped up, trembling and dithering with shock. "What was that firing up the road?"

"I don't know, Ma. Kieran said it might be a— a diversion."

"Oh my God! If they know he's here they'll be down on us like a ton of bricks! How'd he get in here without them'ns seeing him?"

"Angela brought him," Maura said simply.

She and her mother looked at each other.

"She's a wee angel, Ma," said Maura under her breath.

"Sure she is, bless her heart," said Ma. "I need no telling."

She had slotted on her slippers and was pulling her cardigan around her thin body. "But there's nothing she or the whole heavenly host can do for us. I often think the good Lord Himself can do precious little to stop Irishmen fighting."

Ma peeped into Darren's cot and then led the way downstairs. The shooting had stopped and the night was now silent. It was not a peaceful silence, though, but an eerie, waiting silence that frightened Maura almost more than the shooting itself.

In the living-room Kieran was still at the window, but as they came in he turned around and he and Ma looked at each other through the dimness. Then, with a little sound, more like one Foley would make, he stood up and threw himself into Ma's arms.

"What've you done now, you bad boy?" she scolded, but she kissed him before pushing him away from her. She held him at arm's length and looked into his eyes. "What good did you think this bit of madness would do you or any of us?"

Then she began keening and moaning. "Oh, what am I to do? How can a woman manage by herself? Why did your da have to go off with the boyos, with never a thought or a backward look at his family? Not a word from him in months! What do I care for all his high-flown words when it's himself I'm needin' to help and support me—"

She stopped suddenly. They all stood, frozen into silence by the tiny noise they had all heard at the window. A scratching—a tapping—beyond the curtains.

"What's that?" hissed Ma, white as death. "Maura—"

Maura ran to the sofa and tweaked the curtains an inch apart. And there, on the other side of the glass, grimacing urgently to be let in, was a burly, unshaven man in a woolly hat.

Maura turned from the window, caught between dismay and joy.

"Ma! It's him—it's—" She could hardly get the words out.

"Who? Who in the saint's name is it at this hour?"

"It's himself! It's my daddy!"

Fifteen

DA'S ARRIVAL WAS nothing like Kieran's.

Kieran had slipped in like the fugitive he was, but Da, once he was inside the house, behaved as if he were a triumphant general returning from some victory. He fairly swept Maura off her feet, hugged and kissed Ma, embraced Kieran and even gave Angela a pat on the head without really seeming to notice her.

"It's good to be home, so it is!" he kept booming. "Where's the rest of my family? Where's young Foley, where's the tadpole?" He always called Darren that. "And my old Coll, where's Coll? Get them all down here, I want my own around me! It's not every day a man comes home from the wars!"

In vain they all begged him to speak quietly. He was stamping about, shouting and hugging them all. Soon he was calling for some whisky for the celebration and Maura had no alternative but to go and fetch it. But she was glad that Ma and Kieran between them hadn't left much in the bottom of the bottle.

If Kieran had lost weight in prison, Da had put it on while he'd been off with the Provos. He'd always been a big man but now he was fat as well. He seemed to fill the little room with his big body and his big, noisy personality. After the first moments of fright, Maura found this reassuring. He was her daddy, after all—he knew what was what. If he thought it was safe to raise his voice and behave as if nothing in the world were amiss, then it must be.

The watchers outside had gone. Kieran and Da were home. The house once again had grown men in it who knew how to take care of women and children. Maura, pouring out the remains of the whisky into two glasses for her father and big brother, felt the fear and the dreadful burden of responsibility drain away with the last golden drops.

But that feeling was not to last long. Ma was less happy. She let the men toast each other, and the Provos, and the family, and freedom, and a united Ireland, and then throw the whisky (which seemed to Maura very little for so many causes) into the backs of their throats. And then Ma seemed to take charge again, just as if there were no men about at all.

"All right, you've had all there is to drink," she said briskly. "Now sit yourselves down here and get some food inside you to sop it up. Then perhaps we'll get some sense out of one or other of you about what's to be done. Maura, go and heat some soup. No, wait. What about the sausages?"

"They're all gone, Ma. We ate them. Kieran ate most," she added hastily as she saw her mother's expression.

"That's right, I did, and then I sicked them's all up again," said Kieran. For some reason, that made him and Da burst out laughing and throw their arms around each other again.

Ma pursed her lips and folded her arms across her chest.

In all the months Da had been away, Maura hadn't seen that look on her face, that look of impatience that she wore for her well-known tirade against *men*, how useless they were, worse than children and a lot more trouble. . . .

Maura's heart sank when she saw that look. It could only mean that despite all Ma's wailings about how much she wanted Da to come home and take over from her, now that he had, it made no difference. Ma was still in charge.

And looking at Da and Kieran lolling on the sofa, laughing crazily about nothing, Maura realized the truth of it. She remembered, suddenly, that even when Da was at home all the time, it had been like that. Ma only pretended that Da ran things, to keep him sweet.

Maura had learned that trick with her brothers, very early in life. Much as she'd loved Kieran and Patrick and waited on them and given in to them, she had always known deep down that she had to be the responsible one.

Now she went quietly into the kitchen and lit the

gas under the remains of the tinned tomato soup they'd had for dinner. She opened a tin of oxtail to add to it. She felt empty inside. Too much had happened, she couldn't cope with it all. She wished she could be like Coll, shut into her big body, caring, like a cat, for nothing but her own comfort. Not knowing anything or having to worry.

When she turned from the stove with the saucepan in her hand, she found Angela sitting at the table looking at her. Her face had deep shadows on it now, like a much older person's. She had altogether lost that pure and untouched beauty she had had only three days ago. She looked, not as if she had never lived at all, but as if she had lived for years and years, suffering all the worry and guilt and grief that people can feel. It was all there in her deep blue eyes and in the shadows on her face.

"Maura," she said. "I want to say something to you."

"Let me just give the men their soup, or Ma'll be in here after me."

"Yes. Give them their soup," said Angela oddly. "They'll need it."

Maura frowned, but didn't ask what this meant. She put the mugs of soup and some slices of soda-bread on a tray and carried them into the living-room, where Da and Kieran were jawing on ten to the dozen about their adventures. Kieran seemed to have perked right up since Da came. Da was talking at the top of his voice about how he'd determined to come home when he heard on the news that Kiernan was "out," and how word had come that the street was being watched, and how his "group" had arranged the shooting as a diversion so Da could come home and make arrangements to spirit his son away.

"Then should you not be on your way instead of sittin' here gassin'?" asked Ma anxiously.

"Ah, sure, what's the big rush?" asked Da. "In any case we must wait for the car. Listen, they'll never think to look for Kieran *here*. They'll reckon it's the last place he'd dare to come. The bare-faced cheek of him, marchin' in here! What a chip off the old Cuddy block!" and he banged Kieran on the back and beamed at him proudly.

They fell hungrily on their meal and Maura was about to creep back into the kitchen to Angela when her father caught her by the wrist and pulled her onto his knee.

"My little Maurabelle!" he said tenderly, wrapping his big arm around her waist. "You've become a grand big lady since I went off. Have you been a good girl and helped your ma?"

"I'd have gone stark raving mad without her," said Ma shortly.

"Will you go upstairs and bring my Foley and the tad down to see their da?"

"She'll do no such thing!" exclaimed Ma. "At this hour, and with all that's going on—the notion! Why, anything could be goin' to happen at any moment!"

"Nothin's goin' to happen," said Da comfortably, drawing in a mouthful of hot soup with a great slurping sound. "My God, that's a wonderful soup! It's a poor diet we get in the Provos."

"You're evidently not starving," said Ma, drily.

"Sure, we hardly eat a thing."

"Then it must be a liquid diet that's puttin' the fat on you."

"Well, you wouldn't expect men to take the risks we do without some fire in our bellies." He slurped again and jiggled Maura up and down on his knee. She felt intensely nervy and restless. This was crazy. Even if those men had gone off for the moment, they'd be back.

"How are you going to get Kieran away, Da?"

"Now don't you worry your little head about that," he said. "The less you know, the better. Me and the boys will take care of it." He drained his mug. "We'll have him across the border before dawn. You've seen the last of the H-block, son, just take my word for it."

Maura gently dislodged his arm and went back into the kitchen. Angela was sitting just as she'd left her, at the table, but she was doing something rather odd. She had opened one of the small packets of Kellogg's cereal, tipped some of it out on to the table-top, and was eating the Cocopops slowly, one by one.

"What are you doing?"

"Eating these. They're so good. I wish we could have some music. That's what I like best," she said softly. "Eating sweet things and listening to music. "Perhaps those aren't the best things in life, but they're the best I've found so far."

And then she put her head down suddenly on her arms, scattering the Cocopops on the floor.

"Maura . . . I'm frightened!"

"Don't you be," said Maura stoutly, like her father. "There's nothing to worry about now you've brought Da home." She wished she could believe it, but at least she wanted to make Angela feel better. Besides, it frightened Maura to see Angela frightened.

Angela raised a ravaged face and stared at her.

"You trust him? To take care of us?"

"Sure I do!" said Maura loudly.

Angela stood up and began to move restlessly about, her feet crunching the Cocopops on the lino.

"I don't know much yet," she said, "about people. You know him. Perhaps I'm wrong. Oh, I hope so! But I have the most terrible feeling . . ." She stopped near Maura and put her hand on her shoulder, clutching hard. "Listen, Maura. This is what I wanted to say to you. If . . . anything happens . . . I want you to know that I haven't gone far."

"Are you going out again? I wish you'd stop home!"

Angela said nothing for a moment and then just squeezed her shoulder and let it go.

"Nothing is fixed," she said.

"What?"

"Nothing is planned. I've changed things. I shouldn't have, but I did, and that proves nothing is planned. There's no *plan*. Do you understand? Up there. There are rules. Laws. But nothing is fixed. For the future. Angels can't alter things—they mustn't. That's your job."

"Mine? I can't do much!"

"If you can't do anything else, you can always yell."

Maura remembered once at a fair, her da taking her to a gypsy fortune-teller (when Ma's back was turned). The gypsy had told her all sorts of things that were going to happen to her, and although most of them were nice things, Maura had hated it and felt upset all day. Now she knew why. It was the idea that the future was settled, that up ahead were events that you couldn't avoid.

Ma had been livid later, and called it all superstitious nonsense. The relief had been enormous, and it was even more enormous now that Angela had said Ma was right. The future was a blank. Maura smiled for the first time in hours and hours.

"That's good," she said. "Is it a law?"

"It's *the* law," said Angela. Then her eyes opened wide. Without looking around she said quietly, "Here they are, your da's friends. We'd better turn the lights out."

And sure enough, Maura, jumping up, saw shadows and shapes beyond the dark glass in the window and the back door.

Sixteen

MAURA LET THEM in without even asking who they were. If Angela said they were Da's friends, they were Da's friends.

And so they were. There were three of them, all young and tough-looking in dark clothes and pulled-down woollen caps that hid most of their faces. When Maura called to Da and he came through into the kitchen and saw them, his eyes lit up with relief and he hugged two of them and started to say something in his booming voice, but they shut him up with one gesture.

After that, it was all mutterings and closed doors. The five men shut themselves up in the living-room and Ma, Angela and Maura were banished to the kitchen.

"You stay out of harm's way and make some tea," said Da. "Leave men's business to the men."

Ma sniffed, but didn't argue. She made a pot of tea and did a bit of muttering herself. She looked gray-faced with anxiety. Angela went and stood near her but it didn't seem to help. Every little sound made her jump, and once when a door slammed in the next-door neighbor's house she smacked her cup down in her saucer so hard that the handle broke off.

"Oh, Mother of God, will it never end? You could swear they're enjoying themselves while all this goes on. . . . If only they'd listened to me, the pair of them, but it's not a bit of use, they're just hell-bent on having their own mad way. Playing at war like boys and never really knowing what it means, how much pain it costs. Oh God," she cried suddenly, "don't let my man kill anyone! I couldn't bear that."

"Da couldn't," said Maura loudly. "Not my daddy."

"You don't know men." Then Ma's voice lost its keening note and became normal. "Gracious, what's all that mess on the floor?"

Angela gave a guilty start.

"Oh, that was me—I'm sorry. I'll sweep it up."

And she fetched the dustpan and brush and got down on her knees. For the rest of her life, Maura would remember her like that, kneeling there on the cold lino, humbly and ordinarily, sweeping up the Cocopops she had sent scattering in the moment when she had cried out, in that utterly human way, "Maura, I'm frightened!"

Suddenly they heard it, and the hearts seemed to stop in all of them. A noise like the bark of a dog outside. But it wasn't a dog. It was a human voice, barking out an order. And before they could do anything at all, there was a crashing, splintering noise from the hall.

In the next split second came heavy running steps out at the back, the thud of boots as men dropped from the high alley wall. A rifle-butt crashed through the glass panel in the kitchen door, and, before the glass had settled on the floor, the door was flung open.

More men, uniformed men, burst in. The first one thrust Ma aside as they ran through the kitchen. Another bark, louder and closer this time, from the hall.

Ma had leaped to her feet, and so had Angela, the dustpan adding its clatter to the racket of hard boot-steps and shouts and the tinkle of more glass. Maura, half-stunned as she was, thought, *There goes the front-room window—the one overlooking the street*. The next thing, she and Angela were bumping into each other as they tried to rush through the kitchen door at the same moment behind the khaki backs. Angela got through first.

The front door and the door to the living-room had been burst open—the front door was hanging by one hinge. The little hall was crammed with soldiers. Above their heads, Maura could see another, clambering in through the smashed window over the back of the sofa, his rifle barrel catching on the net curtains and dragging them down. Da, Kieran and the other three men were somewhere in there. Trapped. And she couldn't get to them.

She fought, pushing and struggling, but the backs

were too many, too tightly wedged, too strong. She heard her own voice screaming, "Don't hurt my daddy! Da! Da!" and her mother behind her screaming louder, "Don't shoot! Don't anybody shoot!" And the barking voice, still barking, loud unmeaning sounds that only a soldier can understand.

Then the shots rang out—two, almost at the same moment. They exploded in the little house as shatteringly as the bomb had exploded in the street.

Maura's first thought was not of her father or brother, but of Angela, whose delicate ears hated noise. She looked around for her but couldn't see her. Perhaps she'd run upstairs? She turned to look, unaware at first of the complete silence that had fallen. And there, half-way down the stairs, was—Colleen.

Maura stared at her, astounded. She was struggling down the stairs, very quickly for her, holding the bannister with both hands. Her big vacant eyes were wide with the strongest expression Maura had ever seen in them—pure horror.

No one but Maura saw her at first, but by the time she reached the bottom step, there had been a movement in the crush of soldiers. Some had begun to back out of the living-room. They were looking around uneasily at Ma, and Ma, her face a mask, quite blank and chalk-white, moved forward. They made way for her. Maura, without any thoughts in her head, took Coll by the hand and together they walked into the living-room behind their mother.

What Maura had expected to see, she could never

afterwards remember. Perhaps, deep inside her, she had been prepared to see her father or brother stretched out on the floor. She had known that they were wanted men, that their being here in this house tonight put them at risk of their lives.

But they were both standing there in the corner by the television. Keiran was stooping with his hands over his head. Da was upright. He had a big pistol in his hand, and it was shaking. One of the men with him also held a gun. The soldier who had come through the window stood with one boot up on the sofa, his automatic rifle leveled at his hip. The echo of the two shots, and the evil, biting smell of them, was still in the air.

The figure on the floor was Angela.

Everyone in the room was staring at her. The soldiers looked, not terrible and threatening any more, but young and frightened and shocked, as shocked as Da and his friends looked.

Maura's feet were stuck to the ground. She needed to go to Angela but she couldn't budge. It was Colleen who lumbered across the small empty space around the fallen figure and, lowering her heavy body to the floor, heaved Angela up onto her lap.

She bent her head over her and wrapped her big arms around her. Coll's shoulders began to jerk with sobs. She didn't make a sound. Nobody did. The soldiers fell back against the wall. Ma and Da just stood there at opposite sides of the room.

Maura at last found she could move, and ran to Angela's side. She crouched down and touched her white face and stroked her tumbling hair. Her eyelids were closed and her lips were parted. Maura glanced down and saw a little, blood-edged hole in the front of her sweater.

She looked up at the soldiers, her heart suddenly swelling to bursting-point with rage and misery.

"You shot her!" she screamed. "You shot her! You shot my angel and you've killed her!"

At that moment Colleen made a little sound and Maura swiftly turned back to see Angela's eyes opening and a trace of a smile appearing on her lips.

She whispered something.

Maura put her ear close to Angela's mouth.

"That's right." The whisper was no louder than breathing. "When you can't do anything else—yell!" She stopped, and a little frown appeared for a moment on her smooth white forehead. Then she made a motion of her head as if to beckon Maura to listen again. "Don't be sad. I told you. I'm not—going far. I couldn't let Da—shoot anyone—but me, could I?" Her flickering eyes turned to Colleen. "Coll," she whispered urgently. "Moo!"

Coll raised her face, which was streaming with tears. She swallowed. And then she opened her mouth, and out came the purest, sweetest sound, every note true as a bell,

"Alling by un boofinul, all keetern day un Ma—
Alling why un waaaderful, an ol' Go' make un aw!"

She sang a whole verse in her own way and every person in the room listened in absolute silence. And when she had finished she gathered Angela to her heart, with a great, rending sob. Only then did Maura see the other bullet-hole. The one in the back.

That was when the marvelous thing happened, the thing that only she and Colleen saw. It was like the first time when Angel's spirit had been tightly tied to her body but had been struggling to fly free, the time when Maura had heard the whirring of imprisoned wings. Now, in a flash, she saw the angel part of Angela lift itself and float out of the body lying there so still in Colleen's arms.

It was not trapped this time. It rose freely up into the air. Maura couldn't see it clearly, it was too bright, too insubstantial; its outlines dazzled her and she had to shut her eyes. But there were wings, and hands that reached out to touch their faces—Maura's and Coll's—for a moment. Coll, amazed, put up her own clumsy hand to grasp the lovely bright thing, but it was gone. Not flown away; just—vanished. And Maura opened her eyes and looked at Coll, whose face was, for a moment, as bright as a bonfire.

And the tears on both their faces had dried.

Seventeen

WHILE TERRIBLE THINGS are happening, you can never imagine that life will go back to normal, or something like normal. But it does, and in the case of Maura's family, surprisingly quickly.

A week after the soldiers had broken into the house that fearful night, Maura was getting up in the mornings, helping Ma to feed Darren and dress Colleen, getting Foley and herself off to school, just as usual. Because, no matter what they were all feeling, there was just no choice, it had to be like that. And things weren't so very different, after all, on the outside.

Kieran wasn't there, but then, Kieran hadn't been there for two years anyway. He was back in the Maze of course, and he'd lost some remission, but oddly enough not all of it, because the judge took the view that any prisoner will escape if he gets the chance.

The priest he'd tied up and changed clothes with spoke up for him, saying he hadn't been hurt, and had presented a strong temptation to Kieran. Till his escape Kieran had behaved well in prison.

Da wasn't there, but neither had he been around for a while, and here was a funny thing: Ma seemed actually quite relieved that Da, too, was in the Maze, and not running around with the Provos getting up to the dear knew what. Maura understood now that her mother's deepest fear had always been that Da would kill someone, or be involved in bombing, perhaps across the water, and that then he'd be put away for life and that Ma wouldn't be able to feel the same way about him. Angela had understood that, and that was why, when Da raised his pistol to shoot at the soldiers, Angela had thrown herself in his way so that he would "only" kill her.

Maura never blamed Da for Angela's death. The soldier had shot her, too, and it was impossible to know which of them killed her. *And she had chosen to die.* Maura knew now that she had been getting ready to do it, or something like it, all the evening. That was why she had been frightened, that was why she had been eating the Cocopops—a funny way of saying goodbye to life, but it was her way; and she was, Maura decided, more child than angel by then, which made the brave thing she had done all the more wonderful.

Because Da was a bit drunk and hadn't meant to shoot Angela, they only put him in for ten years, which, with good behavior, would be reduced to five.

Ma considered this short sentence, considering everything, "a miracle." Maura knew it was.

Meanwhile, Ma was in charge again, and somehow she seemed stronger than before. She didn't get so tired and she got up at night to see to Darren and in the morning too, so Maura didn't have so much to do. And she was cheerful and comforting and didn't wail so often.

"He's safe enough in there, so he is," she would say. "He'll keep off the whisky and get his figure back, and perhaps they'll let him join the prison choir." She only said this privately to Maura, of course. Prisoners' wives weren't supposed to talk like that, as if they didn't mind their men being inside, and when their relations and neighbors came to commiserate with her, she would rail against the Brits as loud as any of them for locking her poor men up for doing their patriotic duty.

So in one way, the worst thing was that *Angela* wasn't there any more.

Maura missed her with a physical ache. The wonder of having a live angel living with her was only part of what she missed. It was much more the sheer fun and companionship of having a "twin," She knew now that she was meant to have a twin sister, that only the accident of death had robbed them of each other.

But having had a taste, with Angela, Maura found that she could madge her back again quite a lot of the time. She talked to her (aloud, when she was alone, but silently at other times). She wrote notes to her in that funny, twirling writing that she'd now adopted as her own.

But best of all, she dreamed about her, both day-dreams and night-dreams. In the night-dreams. Angela sometimes appeared as her angel-self, and then she didn't talk, and Maura was in awe of her; but in other dreams she would appear as Angela in Maura's old gray sweater and jeans and then they would have adventures together and long, long talks.

Sometimes Maura could remember these in clear detail when she woke up. Often they would be just chats, but at other times Angela would say wise things or give Maura advice, or even tell her off a bit, if she'd done something wrong or silly. Even in dreams Maura was always aware that Angela was an angel and had a job to do and she never resented these tellings-off. They didn't happen often, anyway, because if there was one thing you could say for Maura, it was that she usually did her best.

One very odd thing was that after Angela—the human Angela—had been buried, nobody seemed to remember her or at least mention her. Ma never did. Foley didn't. No one at school said a word, though news of the shooting had been briefly in the papers. Perhaps they were all being tactful about the death of Maura's "cousin." Or maybe . . . maybe Angela's visit, being a miracle anyway, and right outside any normal framework, had just faded from people's minds. Like seeing a vision and then deciding you really hadn't.

But Coll remembered.

Coll *remembered*.

Poor, not-bright Coll, who couldn't even think properly, who had never remembered anything in her life from one day to another, remembered Angela as clearly as Maura did. Maura knew it.

She no longer thought of Coll quite as before. She had shared something entirely beautiful and miraculous with her. And besides, Angela had made her understand that locked away inside Coll's big slow body was a soul like a star, a bright star that never grew dim.

And sometimes when Coll and Maura looked at each other, Coll's blank eyes brightened and she would murmur, "Aaaaang . . ." very lovingly and with, for her, great meaning. She'd hum a few bars of "All Things Bright and Beautiful" in a secretive way. And Maura would say, "That's Angela's music."

"Aaaaang moo," Colleen would say agreeingly. And then, "Soo-ry?"

This, in Coll-talk, meant, not "sorry," but "story." Because Coll listened to stories now, really listened. That, like the Crunchies left by the lolly-tree, had remained, as absolute proof—not that any was needed, for Maura—that Angela, her special angel, had been, for a short while, her special, living friend.

The Best in Children's Literature from

LYNN REID BANKS

I, HOUDINI
70649-0/$4.50 US

THE FAIRY REBEL
70650-4/$4.50 US

THE FARTHEST-AWAY MOUNTAIN
71303-9/$4.50 US

ONE MORE RIVER
71563-5/$3.99 US

THE ADVENTURES OF KING MIDAS
71564-3/$4.50 US

THE MAGIC HARE
71562-7/$5.99 US

ANGELA AND DIABOLA
79409-8/$4.50 US/$6.50 Can

HARRY THE POISONOUS CENTIPEDE
72734-X/$4.50 US/$6.50 Can

MAURA'S ANGEL
79514-0/$4.99 US/$6.99 Can